Misplaced

Misplaced

Here, There, and the Journey Between

A mostly-true story about difficult paths and personal growth

Eric Foster-Whiddon

Foreword by Tracy Reynolds

RESOURCE *Publications* · Eugene, Oregon

MISPLACED
Here, There, and the Journey Between

Resource Publications
An Imprint of Wipf and Stock Publishers
199 W. 8th Ave., Suite 3
Eugene, OR 97401

www.wipfandstock.com

PAPERBACK ISBN: 978-1-6667-0405-1
HARDCOVER ISBN: 978-1-6667-0406-8
EBOOK ISBN: 978-1-6667-0406-8

JUNE 17, 2021

Cover illustration by Daniel J.T. McKay
www.whimwondery.com

To Vanessa
Semper mihi praedilecta

To the Adventure Team
Adam, Chad, Chris, Jimmy, and John
If you want to go fast, go alone.
If you want to go far, go together.

I'm so thankful we walk together.

Contents

Foreword

Good stories tend to read you while you read them. *Misplaced* is such a story. While the narrative and the journey are unique to the author and his traveling companions, the commonality of life choices, intended destinations, internal struggle, hardships, fatigue, mixed motivations, and spiritual ambivalence resonate universally.

Eric Foster-Whiddon's cleverness and deep thoughtfulness are immediately exposed as he characterizes each of his companions with a fictitious name depicting their salient perceived character strengths and their eventual role among the band of brothers sharing the journey "from Here to There." And, while the tale is unashamedly metaphorical and symbolic, his descriptions and story-telling provide ample opportunity to experience the rigors and beauty of the trek. One can almost smell the aromas and visualize the vistas as the hikers follow the blue blazes. *Misplaced* is clearly a good read.

But, if you stop short of internalizing the struggle within, you may miss the greater point and lose the value offered in this brief volume. Reading the narrative is intended as the overture to the symphony or the pregame warmup to the main event. While I have been privileged to know some of the details depicted in *Misplaced* and have the pleasure of understanding much of Eric's heart, it is abundantly clear that his motivation in sharing his journey is for our personal good and potential growth as fellow travelers on planet Earth. As such, the reading of the story is probably not as significant as how we respond to the insights we gain from our own lives as the story "reads our lives." As I ponder the reflection guide I am amazed at the brilliance of many of the questions posed and parallels between the gospel narratives and the story of our misplaced lives. (Be sure to read the epilogue and follow the link to Eric's resource on *Misplaced* and the gospels.) Likewise, it is painfully obvious to me that for us to experience the full potential of *Misplaced*, we must ponder prayerfully and honestly what God may be speaking to our hearts. And, as often is the case in any effective study of a biblical text or response to a masterfully presented sermon, the vital question posed is, "So, what?" What could this mean to me?

I am confident that as you read this provocative tale and experience the essence of a story well told you will find yourself relating and resounding with the greater questions and deeper challenges posed. I love allegories and analogies. And I love both the heart of this writer and celebrate the journey with him. I pray that you, too, will find your place in *Misplaced*.

Dr. Tracy Reynolds
Discipleship Pastor
Grace Fellowship Church
Athens, Georgia USA

Introduction

The tale you will find in the following pages is, as the subtitle states, a mostly-true story about difficult paths and personal growth. The story follows six men on a weekend backpacking trip as they travel a mountain trail along a river. The characters' names are allegorical in the vein of "The Pilgrim's Progress" and "Hinds' Feet on High Places," the influence of which lies barely below the surface of this work. You will follow the journey of the main character, Misplaced, and his interactions with the other men on the trip: Faith, Loyalty, Wisdom, Resolve, and Strength. Each chapter focuses on an interaction between Misplaced and another character, revealing a principle for personal growth while following a difficult path.

There is much about this book that is not, in fact, unique. The leadership and personal growth markets are not lacking in allegorical books. Is there really a need for one more? Even the literary mechanisms employed in *Misplaced* are not novel. More so than the format or literary conventions of the book, the content is also quite commonplace. Everyone faces difficult paths. I would guess that the average person relates well to the journey metaphor; we identify ourselves as pilgrims somewhere between a point of departure and a destination, having left Here and on the way There. In the space between leaving and arriving, you may feel that "misplaced" is an apt adjective to describe yourself.

I hope that the common-ness of this book proves especially beneficial to you. There is a reason that story has been favored as a teaching mechanism since antiquity. Another ancient literary mechanism, the personification of virtues is an effective way to advance the philosophical premises of the story. Most significantly, people ancient and postmodern love an epic journey and identify with the trembling protagonist overcoming obstacles on the way to his destination.

This story is also unique because it is true (mostly). This is the narrative of a hiking trip that changed my life. I was a young business owner withering from self-induced isolation, trying to make sense of the difficulties of entrepreneurship while suffering the withering of my soul in the process. I was invited to spend a long weekend backpacking in northern Georgia (USA). The events of this trip reoriented me, reignited my spiritual life, and rescued my dying business. The characters in the story are real people who subsequently became a brotherhood, a "fellowship of suffering" which we call the Adventure Team. Many years and hiking trips later, we still linger over maps, strategize to shed ounces, and dream of the next journey from Here to There.

Eric Foster-Whiddon
Cambridge, England
January 2021

1

An Invitation to Go There

Standing behind the espresso machine and pulling two shots for himself, Misplaced had quite a weight on his shoulders. He needed more than his usual drip coffee to manage the stress; concentrated caffeine was what this ragged, worried, and weary entrepreneur required. Four ounces of straight espresso was the prescription for today. Letters from the IRS stared at him from the other end of the counter and payroll was coming around the corner. His business both created his caffeine-fueled lifestyle and provided the means to supply it.

The ding of the coffee shop door was followed by the smiling face of his old friend, Loyalty. In the four years before opening the coffee shop, Loyalty and Misplaced spent countless hours talking about their Christian faith and growing families. They were neighbors-down-the-road and frequented one another's homes. When Misplaced and his wife expected their first child, Loyalty assembled a team of friends to help finish the nursery. When his fixer-upper needed a facelift, Misplaced called on Loyalty for help. When Misplaced needed a partner in youth ministry at his church, Loyalty was his right-hand man. When frantically trying to open the coffee shop, threatened with missing a deadline and a much-needed paycheck, Loyalty came to the rescue. They were once very close. Sadly, this was not the case anymore.

In his first two years of business, Misplaced became consumed by his work. As if the 12-hour days weren't enough, his rookie mistakes and mismanagement of the business enslaved him to an even greater degree. During these busy days, Misplaced withdrew from his friends as he tried to make his venture successful. A frequent customer, Loyalty once caught a minute with Misplaced at the coffee shop and expressed his sense of loss regarding his busy brother. "I miss you, Misplaced. You moved into your new house a year ago and I haven't even stepped foot in it." Misplaced's mind was too concerned with anemic bank balances, back-taxes and accounts payable to really feel his friend's sorrow. He smiled and gave a half-hearted "Me too" in response.

This day, Loyalty bounced into the coffee shop with a proposal for Misplaced. "I'm going on a journey from Here to There in a few weeks. It's a three-day hiking trip in the mountains, along a river. All of the guys who are going are men that you know, Misplaced. We have room for one more hiker. Would you like to come along?" Misplaced propped his hands on the top of the espresso machine and stared at the crema that crowned his shots. "I don't need to take three days off of work. I don't need to leave this place. BUT I NEED TO LEAVE THIS PLACE!" he thought to himself. Just a few months earlier, Misplaced had to stop taking a salary from the business and pick up a second job to make ends meet. If he worked hard before, he was working harder now. If he was isolated before, today he might as well have been living on Mars.

"I'm in," he replied.

"Are you sure you'll do it, Misplaced? You backed out the last time I invited you on a trip like this," Loyalty prodded.

"For sure this time. I could use a trip There."

"Great!" Loyalty continued, "I can tell you're worn out, friend. If you're tired of being Here, you have to take a step toward There. Maybe this trip is just what you need."

"What should I do to get ready to go?" Misplaced asked.

"You've done the first thing — make a decision to leave Here and go There. From this point you just need to prepare as best you know how and move in that direction. Here's the thing: you've never been on a trip like this and you don't really know how to prepare. That's OK. Do what you can and you'll have help along the way. You'll figure out the rest as you go. Don't let your apprehension about preparing keep you from going on the journey. You really need to get out of Here, Misplaced."

"More than you know," thought Misplaced. "Sounds good. I'm going, for sure. No backing out this time. I have some friends who have taken journeys like this before; I'll call them and see what I can borrow to get ready. Who should I talk to if I have questions?" asked Misplaced.

Loyalty answered, "I'd call Faith. He has led several trips like this and he planned this one. He can help you get ready."

2

Preparing to Go

The night before leaving to go There, Misplaced spread his borrowed equipment across the kitchen table. "Backpack, sleeping bag, tent . . . what else?" Misplaced talked to himself as he created and checked off his packing list. As a child, one of his prized possessions was an uncle's old Boy Scout Handbook. He read it from cover to cover, studying illustrations of edible plants and tent configurations, but he had been on very few camping trips. He was familiar with canvas pup tents, rectangular sleeping bags, and two-burner camp stoves, but all of that equipment seemed too big for this trip. Whatever he needed, he had to carry on his back from the parking lot to the campsite several miles into the woods. Rummaging through the kitchen cabinets for a water bottle, a question came to mind. "How much water do I need? Is my water bottle big enough?" This seemed like a query for someone with experience, someone who had a few miles under his belt. Misplaced picked up the phone and dialed Faith.

Misplaced made the veteran hiker's acquaintance through the coffee shop. Faith would often come over to get coffee for his wife and the men would chat while the order was being made. He seemed like a nice enough guy and Misplaced enjoyed his interactions with Faith. A tall and slender man, Faith towered almost a whole foot above the average guy. His positive demeanor made it seem as if the unusual height helped him see things from a truly unique perspective. When the world appeared disappointing, Faith was always happy and excited about the future.

"Hello, Faith! Sorry for the last-minute call, but I'm packing tonight and I have a question."

"Don't worry about it! What can I help you with, Misplaced?"

"How much water should I take? I have two aluminum water bottles that I use at the gym. They're about 20 ounces each. Will that be enough?"

Faith explained how to plan for water while backpacking. Another hiker was bringing a filter that would be sufficient for everyone and, since the trail followed a river, water would be plentiful. "Water is one of the most important things you'll need on this journey, but it's also one of the heaviest things you'll carry. Bring both bottles. They'll be enough on this trip because of the river, but on other hikes you might need something more substantial."

Misplaced appreciated Faith's advice, but it was hard for him to ask for it. Though he had no hiking experience and only a vague notion of how to prepare, Misplaced tended to be painfully independent and reticent to ask for help. This independence seemed like a virtue, a manly desire to "take care of himself," but it really was a disguised survival skill that he developed as a boy. A difficult relationship with his stepfather taught Misplaced to avoid criticism by distancing himself from others and figuring things out on his own. He hated for someone to watch over his shoulder as he wrestled with a new concept or skill. "Give me some space, let me do it myself, and judge my work when it's finished," was one of his mantras. He also didn't want to inconvenience anyone by asking for help. This way of thinking betrayed him as he apologized for calling Faith.

"Thank you so much for helping me. I'm really sorry I waited until the night before to call you. I hope I haven't kept you from something important. Thanks again for your time, Faith."

"Seriously, don't worry about it, Misplaced! I'm glad to help."

"Thanks for your willingness, Faith. I'm really excited about this trip, but I guess I'm kinda nervous, too. I've never done something like this. I think I'm most afraid that I'll get out on this journey and realize somewhere between Here and There that I don't have something I need. That would be really bad."

Faith was quick to respond to Misplaced's statement. "Misplaced, you don't completely know what you need because, like you said yourself, you've never done this before. But don't let that stress you out. Prepare the best you can and feel free to ask any questions you have. Just remember that you're not taking this journey alone. There will be six of us on the trail and we're all bringing stuff with us. If there's something you need but don't have, someone else will have it with him . . . for sure! You have more resources than you realize to help you get from Here to There. Seek them out. Don't be afraid to ask for help."

Misplaced and Faith said their goodbyes and hung up. Checking and double-checking his list, the nervous hiker filled his borrowed pack with borrowed gear and hoped that he had all his bases covered. He worried that the journey between Here and There would require tools and skills that he didn't have. Remembering Faith's exhortation, he tried his best to allow his concerns to subside in light of his travelling company. They did a little, but getting from Here to There seemed to be a bigger journey than he could navigate on his own. He was right.

3

Every Step is Going to Hurt

One by one, six very different men found their way to the coffee shop just after lunch on Thursday, packs in tow. These travelers, a mixed bag of would-be hikers, had a strange combination of relationships; some were acquaintances while others were close friends, some were customers while others were businessmen.

Misplaced was a common five-foot-ten, dark-headed, blue-eyed, and hairier than most. He was on the heavy side of average, having lost some thirty pounds over the previous year much to the credit of his friend and fellow hiker, Strength. He was serious-minded and his demeanor could not hide this fact. Any weight he lost around his waist he had gained metaphorically on his shoulders, and folks often misinterpreted his worry for anger.

Also an entrepreneur, Strength changed careers two years prior, leaving the financial industry to become a personal trainer and gym owner. Strength had an academic background in counseling, was passionate about nutrition, and often got into long conversations with Misplaced (which they both enjoyed immensely). Misplaced and Strength found that they had much in common. Both men tended toward being introverts, had large families, and were struggling to see their businesses succeed.

Faith's personality was as big as his towering frame. The elder of the bunch, he was leading the other five men on the same journey he had taken a few years before with a group of boys from his church. Every grey whisker that peppered his short beard had a story behind it, and he was good at telling them. The third entrepreneur in this team of travelers, Faith owned a marketing firm that delivered cookies to customers on behalf of car dealers and realtors after they closed a sale. He and his family lived in a large loft apartment above their business, which was situated on the same picturesque southern courthouse square that was home to Misplaced's coffee shop and Strength's gym.

Faith invited Loyalty on the journey, which required little convincing. If there was a group of people getting together for almost any reason, Loyalty wanted to be there. Include outdoor activities and conversations about God, family, or church and Loyalty considered it a must-attend event. The dirty-blonde, goateed man was a forester-turned-insurance agent and pure joy to be around. He was kind-hearted and witty, responding to every comment with a well-crafted quip. Taller than the other men on the trip but a bit shorter than Faith, Loyalty had the look of a once-was athlete; his muscular frame was softened by the extra twenty pounds he gathered when his workday included less walking through pines and more sitting at a desk. Loyalty grew up on his family's hunting plantation and loved being outside. His career change left him with a longing to be in the woods and he was eager to get on the trail.

As he often did, Loyalty thought of a few friends he wanted to bring along — Misplaced and Resolve. Loyalty didn't know it at the time, but Resolve and Faith had been friends many years ago in high school, and they were an interesting sight to see. If Faith stood "head and shoulders" above the rest, Resolve was power in a small package, a dynamite character on the team. A former Army Ranger, Resolve worked as a mechanical engineer and was passionate about his two young boys. With intelligence and passion to spare, Resolve was known to become hyper-focused on whatever problem needed to be fixed and was near impossible to distract from his chosen cause. Nine months before the trip, Resolve had a titanium plate installed to repair the ankle he broke while roller skating with his boys. His doctor released him to walk on it and said the hike would not be a problem. Resolve was going on this hike, titanium plate or not.

The final member of the ragtag team of hikers was Wisdom, a family practice physician and the doctor for most of the guys on the trip. Thoughtful and reserved, Wisdom exuded intelligence and self-control. He didn't speak often, but when he did his comments reflected his intellect and clever sense of humor. A slight man, Wisdom was more of an athlete than one would expect. He was enthusiastic about theology, politics, and college football. Though this was his first hiking trip, he had researched and prepared so thoroughly that the other men assumed that he had some trail miles under his belt.

Misplaced's café had been designated as the meeting location to load the vans and head north toward the trail. The men exchanged greetings, filled their travel mugs, and threw their gear in the back of the vehicles. "Is that your pack?" Strength asked, poking fun at Misplaced and the equipment stacked and strapped on the outside of his backpack. "Looks kinda heavy." Misplaced snapped back at his friend, "Looks about like yours." Misplaced had left work early to go home and pack the last of his gear. In his rush to finish up and get back to the coffee shop, he was concerned both that he would be late and that he might have prepared inadequately.

Two vehicles, loaded with packs and nervously excited adventurers, embarked on a three-hour drive north to their overnight stop. Wisdom's parents agreed to host the men so they would have a short drive to the trailhead the next morning. His father was a pastor and prepared an evening devotion for the men. He read scripture and talked about how nature displayed God's faithfulness; the men listened and commented in turn. In a previous life, Misplaced would have enthusiastically engaged in such a conversation. However, 3:45AM alarm clocks and working two jobs took their toll and he struggled to stay awake. Wisdom's father asked Faith to close in prayer and the men resigned to their bedrooms. Misplaced was thankful to find his bed.

Misplaced and Resolve were van-mates on the ride to their stopover point. They knew of one another through church affiliation, but had never engaged in any conversation that Misplaced could remember. On the ride up, they talked about typical man stuff, discussing work and gadgets and personal history. They ended up bunking in the same bedroom and talked a little more before they retired for the night. Resolve propped the window open to get a little breeze in the warm room. As he drifted off to sleep, Misplaced was thankful for his new friend.

The men rose early on Friday morning, enjoyed a wonderful breakfast prepared by Wisdom's mom, and headed to the mountains. The roads became narrower and more sinuous as they approached the trailhead. Both vehicles pulled into the large, state-developed parking lot and dropped all of their passengers minus the drivers. The vans pulled away to find the parking lot at the other end. The men planned to leave a van at the trailhead There; they would hike for three days and finish their journey at the van, then drive back to their starting trailhead to pick up the other vehicle and return home. The parking-lot-loiterers waited for what seemed like eternity as the other two men deposited the van and made their way back.

Once the vehicles were in position, the six men strapped on their packs and marched across a bridge to the beginning of the trail on the opposite side of the river. The journey from Here to There had officially begun.

One by one, the men passed a large granite rock engraved with the name of the trail on its face. A few paces past the rock, Misplaced noticed a tree marked with a strip of blue paint. "Those are the trail blazes," explained Faith. "We'll follow them from Here to There. They show up along and along, more frequently when the trail twists and turns through the woods." About the same time that Misplaced saw this first blaze, he also noticed that the muscles in his legs were on fire. "Wow . . . this is going to hurt," he thought to himself as he looked at the rising trail ahead of him. At home, he had imagined this journey as a leisurely stroll through the forest. Somehow he overlooked the fact that he was invited on a "hike through the mountains," which meant lots of ups and downs. Misplaced was thankful that he had gotten back into a running routine, but couldn't help questioning how much fun this journey would really be.

As the hikers meandered along the trail's curves, Misplaced found himself falling toward the back of the line, accompanied by his new friend Resolve. Misplaced brought up the rear because he wasn't accustomed to hiking. Resolve, however, moved slowly because of his ankle injury. In fact, he had become quite the efficient hiker while serving as a Ranger and had countless stories of navigating jungles for days at a time with his soldiers. Misplaced was finding that Resolve was quite the interesting fellow, full of unique and strongly-held opinions. Misplaced admired Resolve's willingness to communicate his beliefs, regardless of how unusual or unpopular they may be. He was comfortable with being different, and Misplaced found Resolve refreshing.

Making trail conversation, Misplaced asked Resolve how he broke his ankle. After Resolve shared the details and described the surgery, Misplaced couldn't help but ask, "How does it feel to hike with that titanium plate?" Resolve's answer struck Misplaced with its honesty and underlying truth. "It hurts, but I knew it would. I made up my mind before I came on this hike that every step would be painful. But there are some long, hard, beautiful miles between Here and There, and I wanted to see all of them. It's that way with any journey like this, even if you're not injured. The only way to cover all those miles is to take one more step . . . even if it hurts."

As they walked along, Misplaced pondered Resolve's impressive character and the truth he shared. The further he hiked down the trail, the further away his problems seemed to be. Faced with the fact that the journey would be harder than he anticipated, Misplaced still found his spirits rising as he followed the trail. With each step through the green wilderness, he felt a peace return to his soul that had been missing for years. Misplaced was grateful for this journey, no matter how difficult it would prove to be.

4

Sixty Pounds . . . and Then Some

As they hiked through the trees, the men naturally separated into pairs. Strength and Wisdom were quick-footed and led the procession. Faith kept conversations stoked along the trail and tended to float in the middle of the line, sometimes pushing toward the front to chat with the faster men, sometimes dropping back to join the conversation with Resolve and Misplaced. When the hikers first left the trailhead, Loyalty walked along in the middle with Faith, but he lost more ground with every uphill climb. Eventually, Misplaced and Resolve were on his heels. The trail rose to a ridge with wooded valleys on either side and Loyalty struggled to the top. "Guys, I need to stop a minute and take off this pack!" The men gathered along the trail. Some unbuckled their backpacks, some left them on. Loyalty dropped his pack and crumpled to the ground, huffing and sweating.

"How heavy is your pack, Loyalty?" Faith questioned.

"Well, I may have overpacked a little. It's sixty pounds . . . and then some." Loyalty answered.

"Wow! What did you bring?" "What is in there?!?" "That's a LOT!" Novice hikers, all of the men packed heavier than necessary. However, Loyalty's pack topped the scales.

"All the normal stuff . . . my tent, sleeping bag, inflatable pad, cook set, food, water. Oh, and my extra clothes, playing cards, back massager, pistol, and . . . "

"What is THAT?!?" Resolve exclaimed. "Just my toothpaste." Loyalty held up the family-sized tube for everyone to see. After the men chuckled at Loyalty's excessive hiking gear, they took turns naming things they brought themselves that weren't worth the effort to lug up the mountain. All of the heavy extras seemed necessary at home, but the trail was proving otherwise. While they rested, the men enjoyed some snacks and were soon ready to mount their packs and walk a little farther.

The men started the trail in the late morning hours and found it blanketed with a mixture of shadows and sunshine as the light fell through the canopy. The path dropped to wooden footbridges that crossed babbling mountain streams. It rose to run along the edge of the mountain, pausing at rock formations that peeked out of the forest. The vistas invited the hikers to linger and gaze at the acres of woodland that rolled as far as the eye could see, like a fuzzy green blanket concealing a giant's knobby knees beneath. As the men reached each new overlook, Wisdom, Faith, and Strength would press on down the trail, barely looking up. Misplaced mumbled to Resolve and Loyalty, "I didn't come up here to just keep walking. I'm going to stop and enjoy the view!" Though he wanted to take in the moment, Misplaced truly needed the oxygen more than the scenery and was happy to use the vista as an excuse to rest.

As the men marched along through the forest, Loyalty continued to fall further and further behind. Strength and Wisdom had gotten into the habit of stopping along the trail and waiting for the others to catch up, making sure that everyone was accounted for safely. At one such stop, the men had been gathered for a few minutes and there was still no sign of Loyalty.

"When was the last time you saw him?" Wisdom asked Misplaced and Resolve. "It's been awhile," Resolve replied. "He was right behind us for a long ways, but I don't remember seeing him after the last couple of turns in the trail." It was apparent that Loyalty was having a difficult time with the pace and elevation change of the hike. He was stopping frequently for breath and water, often commenting with frustration about his struggle.

"He's really having a hard time," Misplaced declared.

"Has anyone heard a whistle?" Wisdom asked. All of the men had loud, high-pitched emergency whistles attached to their shoulder straps for use in case someone was hurt or separated. The men stopped talking to listen; no one heard anything except the sounds of the forest and their own elevated heartbeats.

"Guys, maybe someone should go check on him. Remember, he brought a pistol!" Strength joked, exaggerating Loyalty's desperate, out-of-shape condition.

After the short round of laughter died, Wisdom commented, "Seriously though, we need to find out if he's OK. I'll head back down the trail and find him. You guys stay here and listen for me. If there's a problem, I'll blow my whistle."

The men agreed that this was a good idea, and Wisdom set off to find their lost friend. The remaining hikers talked quietly and took the opportunity to rest and refuel. Almost fifteen minutes later, Wisdom and Loyalty came around the corner, walking slowly but otherwise seeming to be in good spirits.

"Are you OK?" the men asked their winded friend.

"I'm fine, just moving slowly. I had to stop a couple of times to rest and got further behind you guys. I'm not used to being the most out-of-shape guy on the trip!"

This statement struck Misplaced. He had not really noticed the weight that Loyalty had put on, nor thought about the sedentary nature of his new job. Misplaced attended a camping trip that Loyalty organized five years earlier. The trip included a short day hike to a waterfall, and Misplaced remembered how he struggled to make the walk into the woods while Loyalty strode along without hindrance. The men did not take backpacks on that hike, but Misplaced was carrying an extra thirty-five pounds as the result of sodas, honey buns, and a myriad of bad health decisions. All these years later the tables had turned and Misplaced found himself saddened by his friend's struggle.

After Loyalty had a moment to rest, the men donned their backpacks and struck out down the trail, being more careful to keep an eye on their slow-footed friend. Thankfully, the trail fell to a bottom with a long stretch of flat walking, eventually finding its way to the river's bank. After enjoying a moment by the water, the men followed the trail up and away from the river. The path made a hard left turn and the hikers found themselves peering up a steep incline. The trail looked like a dirt ruler, marked at intervals by small wooden logs that crossed from one side to the other at a slight angle. These logs created steps up the trail, but their primary purpose was not to serve as forest stairs. These fixtures were turn-outs, designed to redirect rainwater into the woods and keep it from washing the trail's soil to the bottom of the hill.

As the men followed the trail straight up the mountain, Misplaced discovered that the turnouts were great places to stop and rest when his legs burned and his lungs felt like exploding. He plodded upward, trying his best to keep moving as sweat streamed off the end of his nose. Finding himself just behind Faith, he looked to see Resolve resting with Loyalty at a turnoff several yards behind him. Misplaced turned his focus back to the rising trail and trudged past a few more turnouts. As he rested and fought for breath, he looked back to check on the progress of his friends. Misplaced was surprised to find that they seemed to have only moved one turnout further up the trail, two at the most.

Quite a few painful steps later, Misplaced was relieved when the path turned to the right and settled into a much less aggressive uphill trajectory. He walked slowly, waiting for Loyalty and Resolve to make it past the last turnout. Misplaced stopped on the trail and waited for his friends to catch up. When they did, Loyalty kindly cursed the incline and shared his strategy with Misplaced. "I was dying," he said. "I literally had to stop at every turnout to rest. I would tell myself, 'Just make it to the next turnout . . . then you can stop!' I honestly didn't know if I would make it to the top. If that incline had been any longer, you would have had to go There without me. You'd have to leave me out here by myself; I couldn't take one more step up!"

The men followed the trail over a ridge and around the edge of a bottom. As it rose along the side of the mountain, it snaked through a patch of large-leaved trees growing beneath the towering pines and hardwoods. Misplaced, Resolve, and Faith paused their hike to eat some snacks and take a break. After dropping their packs and weary bodies to the ground, Loyalty spoke up. "Misplaced, I'm proud of you. You're doing a great job on this hike! I remember when we went on that camping trip so many years ago and you struggled to make it to the waterfall, WITHOUT a pack! Now you're out-hiking me!"

Misplaced was proud of Loyalty's acclamation but didn't want to show it. Instead, he retorted, "That's kind of you but it's not really a big deal. I'm proud of you for sticking with it even though you're having such a hard time." Loyalty's response took Misplaced by surprise. "Yeah, it's no secret that this trip is kicking my butt. I'm pretty frustrated with myself for getting in this kind of condition. But just because I'm struggling doesn't mean I can't celebrate your successes."

If he was honest with himself, Misplaced would have to admit that Loyalty's perspective was perplexing. How could someone be so encouraging when he was struggling so badly on his own? Traditionally, Misplaced had been overcome by his own shortcomings and fears. He seemed to wear his emotions on his sleeve, and there was no disguising his anger and frustration when he felt that he was failing. Another survival skill from his childhood, Misplaced was quick to distance himself from others when he thought that he was performing poorly. However, Loyalty seemed to be doing the opposite. He did not withdraw from his friends in his struggles; instead, he relied on their help and encouragement, even carrying on conversations in the midst of his pain. "Why am I so quick to pull away from folks?" Misplaced asked himself. "I wish I could be more like Loyalty. I get so tired of feeling alone. If I pushed a friend away every time I struggled or failed, I would eventually end up without any." Misplaced's internal dialogue reminded him of friendship after friendship that had been abandoned when relating became difficult or he felt inadequate or threatened. Watching Loyalty's struggle to keep moving was inspiring for Misplaced and made him thankful that his old friend was so persistent, intentionally staying connected despite Misplaced's efforts to isolate himself.

"He'll make it, one way or the other," Misplaced thought. Though neither man realized it, Loyalty's dedication to conquer the mountain motivated Misplaced to do the same, even though he was carrying some extra "baggage" of his own. The further he walked through the woods, the more thankful he was that he was surrounded by able companions. "I wouldn't be on this trip if Loyalty had not invited me . . . and I doubt I would get There if I was trying to do it alone." Like most journeys, this one was not meant to be traveled in isolation. Despite his introversion, Misplaced was glad to be walking with friends.

5

Adapt and Overcome

The men followed the trail as it danced between the river and the forest for several miles. Legs were beginning to tire, shoulders ached, and the hikers were ready to become campers for the evening. After passing two smaller settlements, the trail wound its way out of the dense forest and into a spacious campsite near the river. "Want to stop here, guys? This looks like a good spot," asked Faith. One by one, the men dropped their packs and found places to sit and rest their weary feet. Though this was the inaugural hiking trip for most of the guys, they all had camping experience and knew that the most important duties included setting up shelter and gathering wood for a fire. The men scattered, searching for flat spots and dry logs. After a few moments of scrambling among the trees, Strength walked back from the other side of the trail. "Hey guys! There's a better spot over here. Come check it out!" The men left their packs and followed Strength to see what he discovered. Just a few yards away, he had found a more spacious campsite on the same side of the trail as the river. A circle of large stones served as a fire ring with logs pulled alongside for campers to lounge and tend to the fire. Previous occupants had left some unused firewood nearby. At the edge of the river, the ground dropped steeply to the fast-moving water. The river was beautiful and fairly wide here, providing easy access to filter water for drinking and cooking. "This looks great!" "Let's set up here!" "Awesome!" The men were enthusiastic about their new site and hurried back across the trail to gather their gear and relocate.

Backpacks spilled their contents on the ground as the men began to set up camp. Each traveler had a slightly different setup; tents of varying shapes, sizes, and colors popped up all around. Misplaced constructed his borrowed one-man backpacking tent. Easy enough to set up, it looked like an orange dirt dauber's nest on the ground; just barely long enough for an average man, rising knee height off the ground with an opening just at one end. As he filled the tiny tent with sleeping gear, Misplaced realized that it had no room for his pack. "I guess I'll just hang the pack from a tree," he determined. As he hunted a perch for his backpack, Misplaced noticed that one of the men's setup was remarkably different from the others. Resolve had no tent; he was stringing a hammock between two trees with the fire ring on one side and the river on the other.

"Are you sleeping in that?" Misplaced asked, intrigued by Resolve's idea. "Yep. I've spent many a-night in a hammock in the woods," Resolve replied. Upon further questioning, Misplaced learned that Resolve had quite a history with hammock camping. After finishing his service with the Army Rangers, his new friend lived for two years in a state forest while attending college. "My hammock was my bed. I sleep better like this than I do at home."

Resolve's hammock didn't look like the ones Misplaced had seen in backyards over the years. Instead of rope woven together, this hammock was made from a thin piece of fabric gathered together at the ends and tied with rope. Above the hammock, Resolve strung a sheet of clear plastic and pitched it like a tarp. He had not even brought a conventional sleeping bag; instead, Resolve had a blanket to keep him warm as he slept.

Just as each man's campsite was going up, the sun was going down. The pile of wood by the fire ring grew considerably as the men scrounged up more fuel. Faith started the fire while Wisdom filtered enough water for everyone to use for supper. Resolve and Faith fired up their tiny backpacking stoves and began boiling water for the men to add to ramen noodles and dehydrated meals.

Still early in the evening, the sun seemed to set more quickly in the woods than it did otherwise. As the forest grew darker, the campfire grew brighter and the men chatted as they ate dinner. In any other setting, the backpacking food would have left something to be desired. At the end of their first day of hiking, the rehydrated meals were welcomed by exaggerated appetites.

The men cleaned up from supper and sat by the campfire for several more hours. The conversation primarily revolved around their personal histories and careers. Misplaced was intrigued by Faith's business; selling cookies as thank-you gifts from car dealers and realtors seemed like such a creative idea. Faith shared his entrepreneurship story; how he left a previous employer to start his own business, nearly failed in the early years, acquired a well-matched business partner and found an upward trajectory for his company. His tale was full of familiarity for Misplaced, who felt as if he was walking the same path but had not quite made it to the "upward trajectory" part.

As the night lingered on, the men learned first-hand why 9PM is called "hiker midnight." The forest was so dark that it felt like the deepest part of the evening and the exhausted hikers were fighting to stay awake. Misplaced was tired but reluctant to go to bed. On the previous camping trip with Loyalty he discovered the peace that comes with "unplugging" from the world, only being concerned with what happened within the campfire's circle of light. Misplaced found much joy in tending the fire, rubbing the bottoms of burning logs to knock off charred wood and expose fresh fuel. Though they did not express the fact, no one wanted to be the first man to turn in for the evening, triggering a domino effect that would officially mark the end of the first day. When he could not fight it anymore, Wisdom stood up and announced his retirement. "I'm beat, guys. Heading to bed. See you in the morning!" One by one, the men followed suit and found their spots for the evening. After stowing away his cook set and changing into sleeping clothes, Misplaced wiggled his way into the dirt dauber tent and attempted to get comfortable. Thankfully, exhaustion overcame the discomfort of the hard ground and Misplaced drifted off to sleep.

Morning came quickly and Misplaced couldn't decide if he stirred early because of the rising sun, his sore muscles, or the tenacity of his internal clock. Since taking a second job, Misplaced had been waking up long before daybreak to exercise before his twelve-hour workday began. He had never suffered from sleeping problems, but the stress of owning a business kept him awake for more nighttime hours than he cared to number. These days, Misplaced had a hard time going back to sleep once he stirred. He lay uncomfortably on the ground and dozed in and out of sleep, listening for the rustling of other hikers. When he finally heard zippers and footsteps, Misplaced left the warmth of his sleeping bag and writhed out of the little tent.

After stretching and regaining his bearings, Misplaced surveyed the campsite to take inventory of his friends. As is the custom on camp mornings, conversations began with, "How'd you do last night?" This morning, the question was unnecessary in Resolve's case; Misplaced found him lying on the ground instead of in his hammock, indicating a less-than-stellar night of camping. "What happened, Resolve? Did you fall out of your hammock last night," Misplaced asked, with no intent to poke fun. "No. I got cold in the hammock. The air underneath me was sucking the heat out of me and I figured I would be more comfortable sleeping on the ground next to the fire than in my hammock and freezing to death."

Faith stoked the campfire again and the men gathered around to prepare their breakfast. In just a few minutes, water was boiling and the men were rehydrating scrambled eggs, oatmeal, and such. The token coffee snob, Misplaced pulled out one of his backpacking "luxury" items — a plastic single-cup coffee maker. As the other guys poured instant coffee into hot water, Misplaced spooned scoop after scoop of gourmet coffee into his gadget and filled it with boiling water. He was surprised how awkward such a simple and familiar task seemed in the wilderness. He was accustomed to utilizing flat workspaces, water with exact volumes and temperatures, even scales and timers to create a perfect cup of hand-brewed coffee. In the woods, he fought to set up his caffeine lab on a log and "eyeball" his coffee measurements. This environment magnified even small challenges and he found that the less-than-ideal circumstances added frustration and a margin for error that he did not appreciate.

When Misplaced pulled out his brewer, Loyalty laid claim to the second cup. He was happy to provide a little cup o' joy for his friend, but the pressure of preparing decent coffee in the wilderness caused Misplaced's stress level to rise. He knew how much Loyalty enjoyed coffee and Misplaced wanted to deliver for his friend. Once again, he felt like a kid struggling to make something work while others watched over his shoulder. Surely they were critiquing his processes. Certainly they noticed how he fumbled and fought with something so simple. There was no doubt that they questioned his coffee skills and his credentials as the local coffee expert. As his friends sipped instant coffee from their anodized aluminum camp mugs, Misplaced could feel their judgmental stares burn into his back as he fought with a brewing mechanism that was so simple, so measured, so repeatable . . . in a controlled environment at home. Once he got the boiling water poured into the brewer and checked the time on this watch, he turned to face his critics . . . who were busy cleaning up breakfast paraphernalia, seemingly unaware of his coffee crisis.

After a painfully long two-and-a-half minutes, Misplaced poured up Loyalty's coffee and apologized for what he was sure would be a lackluster cup of java. "I'm sure it'll be good, Misplaced. It has to be better than instant coffee! I'm just glad you brought the good stuff."

Cleaning up cook sets turned into cleaning up camp, and the men shoved tents and sleeping bags and clothes back into their packs. Misplaced watched as Resolve took down his hammock setup. Though Resolve had a disappointing night, the idea of using a hammock for camping intrigued Misplaced. The idea hinted at a near-impossibility that captured his imagination: could sleeping at camp be truly comfortable?

While in college, a roommate invited Misplaced to run with him for exercise. He agreed to come along, certain that it would be a short-lived attempt. Surprisingly, Misplaced found that he enjoyed the exertion, repetitive motions, solitude, and clarity of thought that his runs provided. He began to run regularly and lost a considerable amount of weight. However, his new sport also triggered chronic lower back pain and threw him into a cycle of activity, injury, and recovery that continued off and on for ten years. Misplaced would wake up every morning sore and stiff after sleeping in his own bed. Getting up after "sleeping" through the night on the forest floor was exponentially worse.

For years Misplaced wanted a hammock for his backyard but had never bought one. Somehow the gathered-end, fabric hammock that Resolve used seemed to promise a camping experience that would be much more enjoyable than what Misplaced had just endured. "I am already so sore and tired after hiking all day; I don't want to wake up sore from sleeping, too. There has to be a better way than sleeping on the ground," he thought to himself. As Resolve was packing up his hammock and tarp, Misplaced approached him.

"Do you really sleep better in the hammock than you do at home?"

"Usually, yes. That's why I was able to live in the woods for those years . . . the hammock is really comfortable once you get it dialed in. My problem is that I'm always tinkering with stuff and changing my setup. I guess it's the engineer in me. I change stuff trying to make it better, but changing stuff also opens me up to failure. But I can't stop doing it," Resolve responded.

"A journey like this has so many challenges and discomforts that you can't avoid. Between my body being sore and tired, dealing with the elements, fighting with gear . . . it would be awesome if I could at least get good sleep."

"You're thinking in the right direction, Misplaced. Yes, there are difficulties that you cannot avoid on this kind of journey. You simply have to endure them. In the Rangers, one of our mottos was to 'adapt and overcome.' We have to do a lot of that on the trail. If you can remove some unnecessary difficulties, you'll have more stamina to overcome the ones you have to face. But to remove those challenges, you sometimes have to think beyond the usual expectations, to try stuff that is outside of the norm. When people think of camping, they think of tents. But if you ask most folks how they sleep in a tent, the answer is not usually very positive. So why not try something different?"

"Yeah, it's that old 'But we've never done it that way,' rut that folks get into. If you keep doing the same things, you keep getting the same results. If I keep sleeping in a tent because that's what you do when you camp, then I'll keep sleeping poorly and waking up sore. I really want to try and change that." Misplaced liked the way his new friend was willing to challenge established norms.

"Misplaced, I really think you can figure out how to have a better camping experience. It just takes some research and testing, some trial and error. Be willing to do something different and something you endure can become something you enjoy."

As Misplaced finished packing his gear, the conversation with Resolve turned over in his mind. "There has to be a better way," he thought to himself.

Think beyond expectations.

Try something new.

Reduce unnecessary difficulties.

Conquer unavoidable difficulties.

A creative person, Misplaced easily found meaning in symbols and metaphors. His journey was beginning to take on a deeper significance than just a weekend in the woods. He knew that he had proverbial mountains waiting for him at home, just like he had literal mountains waiting for him down the trail. Some of the difficulties that these mountains introduced into his life could not be avoided, but he was certain there were ways he could reduce the pain and stress in his life. He had to try something different. Misplaced was finding some new inspiration for his journey. He was beginning to believe that he could adapt and overcome.

6

Almost to the Top (Again)

Loaded up and enthusiastic about a new day on the trail, the six hikers left camp and headed deeper into the forest. The men spread out along the path and conversations ensued as they separated into pairs. The faster men hiked together at the front of the line, the slower ones at the back, and the others in between. This is normal when hiking in large groups; hikers pair off according to speed. As the morning stretched on, the distance between the groups shortened and lengthened. At times, all six men could be seen along flat stretches or while climbing a long, slow incline. When the trail twisted and turned through the forest, the hiking pairs would often be separated by as much as a hundred yards and hundreds of trees. Especially during difficult ascents, even the pairs would be broken up and the hikers felt like six men on solo backpacking trips who just happened to be in the same forest at the same time. Conversations would cease as the men focused their mental and physical resources on simply breathing, taking another step, and trying to enjoy their surroundings in the process.

Some men powered through the uphill climbs but struggled with the slow, punishing impact of the downhill descents. Wisdom particularly despised going downhill. He and a few others found that jogging down the mountain was more forgiving than plodding and constantly "riding the brakes." The risk of turning an ankle was one they were willing to take. Others became winded while marching uphill and had to stop often to breathe and relieve burning legs. These hikers celebrated every time the trail crested a ridge and began to fall toward a bottom on the other side. A few of the men were pretty comfortable regardless of whether the trail rose or fell. To his own surprise, Misplaced found himself in this category.

The trail flirted with the river for mile after mile. The path would run close to the water, then rise to a high shoulder, then leave altogether for a half mile or more. As it wound back into the woods and away from the water, the trail would often drop to cross smaller creeks that ran down the mountainside, eventually finding their way into the rushing current far below. Wooden footbridges had been installed to help wanderers cross the creeks. Though they were not torrents, the tributaries were significant enough to make things difficult and the high, dry passage was appreciated. Trying to cross the creeks without a bridge would have surely ended in wet feet or worse.

When the trail returned to the shoulder high above the river, the hikers walked out of the dappled shadows and enjoyed the direct morning sunshine for a few yards at a time. As they ventured deeper and deeper into the backcountry, they found sections of trail that were obviously less frequented than the miles closer to the trailhead and parking lot. In areas, vegetation threatened to swallow the trail. Occasionally a metal diamond could be found nailed to a tree. "Those must be old blazes," Misplaced thought to himself. It appeared as though the trail had once used the diamonds for navigation but had replaced them with less expensive and more traditional painted blazes. Along the deeper and less easily accessed sections, the occasional metal blaze had been missed when the trail maintenance teams were replacing them with paint. "That could get really confusing," the newbie hiker thought to himself.

As the morning crept along, each hiker settled into his own pace along the trail. Misplaced spent quite a bit of time hiking by himself and thinking. He did lots of thinking, no matter where he was. While in college years ago, one of his best friends commented, "Misplaced, I don't think I've ever met anyone with more internal dialogue than you! You remind me of the narrator from 'The Wonder Years.'"

Misplaced spent his early childhood without siblings and had no problem playing by himself. He grew up in a time when parents relegated kids to the yard for the entire day. Misplaced would entertain himself by rummaging and exploring and creating. His family lived in a pecan grove, and his most ambitious boyhood goal was to climb every tree in it. Some were easy, with low-hanging limbs. Others required ladders which he made from scrap wood nailed to the trunks. Misplaced spent his days building space-age communication devices from old bicycle parts, shooting bottle rockets at his grandmother's cows, and roaming through the scattered stands of pines on the family farm. The remnants of past childhood adventures were hidden in unexpected places. His mom was the only daughter in a family of five children, and the farm had been his uncles' boyhood wonderland, too. Words painted in the loft of the old hay barn proved that some other boy liked to climb in the rafters, just like him. Near the ferring house, the remains of an old dirt bike could be found just below the topsoil. When Misplaced played there, he was transformed into an archaeologist on a history-making dig. What possessed his uncle to bury a motorcycle? Apparently he had wrecked it and wanted to hide the evidence from his father. Surely his dad wouldn't notice that the machine was missing altogether . . .

As Misplaced hiked alone, he found that he settled into a rhythm of sorts. Breathe in, step, step, breathe out, step, step, step, repeat. Other than the occasional bird, his steps and labored breathing were the only sounds he heard. The monotonous rhythm became a meditative experience and his thoughts were free to wander the corners of his mind while he wandered the forest. As his body struggled to climb the next hill, his mind struggled with questions like, "How did I find myself at this place in life?" "Am I doing what I'm designed to do?" "Will my business survive?" "Am I being negligent by spending a weekend in the woods and not at work?"

Before becoming an entrepreneur, Misplaced was a vocational minister. He became a Christian at sixteen while at a weekend church camp. He remembered that pivotal morning in a little Methodist chapel out in the country. A minister gave a short sermon, there was some worship time, and the camp counselors "opened the altar" for prayer. Misplaced felt no overwhelming spiritual crisis that moved him to pray at the altar. In fact, the whole experience seemed a little underwhelming. Even at sixteen, Misplaced felt the weight of the world on his shoulders. What should he do about college? Choosing a career? Finding a wife? How was he going to survive a difficult relationship with his stepdad? Was he ever going to know his biological father? In that moment, Misplaced felt that God was offering him a chance to give up, to stop making his own decisions, to completely surrender. The invitation to "deny yourself and take up your cross and follow [him]" was welcomed, even though it felt less like spiritual victory and more like acquiescence... or forfeiting... or death. In all honesty, Misplaced didn't really care if he was giving up or not. Under a weight that seemed too great for his teenage heart to bear, Misplaced gladly accepted the invitation to lay down his life and follow. He agreed to start a journey that he knew almost nothing about and was totally unprepared to complete. That weekend, he decided to put one spiritual foot in front of the other and see where it led.

As memories tumbled around in his head, Misplaced looked up the trail as it rose higher and higher. He remembered the time he untied the wrong end of a rope when helping his uncle remove some cargo from the top of his vehicle. "That's not how you untie this, Misplaced. That's the smaller knot, but it's not the one you take loose. Don't take the path of least resistance." He had never heard that phrase before, but it made sense to him and burned itself into his mind. In the following years, Misplaced found that he tended to choose the path of most resistance. The dirt trail he followed as he trudged up the mountain seemed to embody his tendencies in life.

He chose to be a Christian.

He chose to abstain from sex, alcohol, drugs, and partying as a teenager.

He chose to be a musician and a minister, both of which provide a meager living.

He chose to marry a woman who had a young daughter.

He chose to live in a "fixer-upper."

He chose to homeschool his oldest child.

He chose to build an enormous youth ministry.

He chose to drive his youth group half-way across the country for a summer camp.

He chose to meet with men for one-on-one discipleship.

He chose to leave church staff.

He chose to open a coffee shop in a town where coffee shops fail, on a downtown square that was dying.

Now he chose to walk up a mountain and call it "recreation."

Why did Misplaced make the choices he did? Because when he was sixteen, he gave up. He found a new identity as a follower of Christ, and though some might call him a fool he believed God would direct his steps. He learned to study scripture, to pray, and to listen for the voice of the Holy Spirit to guide him in his decisions. He became familiar with the struggle of discerning God's will while being tempted to follow his own. Looking back, Misplaced could easily identify decisions that were certainly more influenced by his own desires and not so much by the Spirit. However, he was confident that most of his major decisions were directed by the Lord, especially his decisions to become a Christian, serve as a minister, and marry his wife.

Though he was beginning to despise it, he knew that opening his business was on that list.

When the idea to start his business first emerged, Misplaced and his wife wrestled with it, trying to determine its source. They talked and prayed and sought counsel. They did the spiritual heavy lifting until they came to the conclusion that this new direction was, indeed, from the Lord. Just as clearly as Misplaced heard God call him into ministry, he heard his call into entrepreneurship. He was certain that God had a plan. Just as Jesus instructed his disciples to climb into a boat and go to the other side of a sea that would toss them and test their faith, Misplaced knew that God had called him to follow this path through unknown trials and difficulties.

There were times that being an entrepreneur was very rewarding. At other times, it seemed to come with a price tag that was entirely too high to pay. There were times that Misplaced felt like he was succeeding, only to be followed by moments when he felt like a complete failure. Mornings were filled with hope and nights were filled with despair. Some days, Misplaced was overwhelmed with thankfulness for the blessings that his business provided for his family. At the end of long days or working weekends, he cursed the coffee shop and accused it of robbing from his children.

There were days when Misplaced felt that entrepreneurship was a perfect fit. There were other days when he felt very . . . well, misplaced.

Though he loved the Lord and trusted his leadership, Misplaced was having a serious crisis of faith. He knew that God had led him to open his business, but his business was failing. Misplaced owned his mistakes and shortcomings as a manager, but he could not see the light at the end of the tunnel. Was the store destined to fold? If God led Misplaced to open the business, did he also intend for it to fail? Could it be that Misplaced needed a lesson in failure? Does God's leadership always imply success? What is success, anyway?

At the base of these questions, Misplaced was really asking, "Is God good? Can I really trust him? What happens if I fail?"

Misplaced had followed God for almost twenty years, through every twist and turn along life's path. In the middle of the forest, Misplaced found himself wondering if his choice to follow Jesus had been a good one. He was unhappy with where he was and what his life had become. Was he still content to "give up," to allow God to call all the shots?

Daylight burned and early morning became late morning. Soon, the men had logged nearly five miles and it was almost time for lunch. Temperatures were still fairly cool, but the exertion of the morning hike left Misplaced red-faced and sweaty. He was surprised how his heart rate remained elevated for such long periods of time. He had to stop frequently to reach his water bottles and take a drink. During these short moments of rest, his pulse barely dropped. "If you're supposed to get your heart rate up for 20 minutes a day, I think I'm good for the next month after this trip!" he thought to himself.

He followed the trail as it turned sharply and found that he had caught up with Wisdom and Strength, lounging in the shade of the low branches and wide leaves of a stand of rhododendrons. Wisdom invited Misplaced to join them. "We're stopping for lunch. Take a break and eat with us!"

Misplaced dropped his pack and plopped down next to his friends. He looked like he was headed to work out, hiking in tennis shoes, athletic shorts, and a t-shirt from Strength's gym. His appearance caught Strength's attention. "I've gotta say, Misplaced, that I'm impressed with how well you've done on this hike. You've really kept up. What are you doing to stay in shape?"

Misplaced described himself as a "serial starter" at the gym. He had a tendency to work out for two or three months very steadily. As he was beginning to see results, he would inevitably drop off just long enough to erase all of his progress. Misplaced would blame it on changes in his schedule or busy-ness at work, which would be mostly true, but his lack of consistency caused him to have to start over . . . and over . . . and over. This hike came during an "off season" from the gym, and Strength was surprised that Misplaced wasn't dying on the side of the mountain.

"I've been running a lot. That's probably it." Misplaced answered. Changing the topic, he made an observation that plagued him all morning. "Have you guys noticed that when you're hiking uphill, you're sure you see the top of the mountain and you're almost there. Then you get to that spot and realize there's more climbing up ahead? That's happened to me ALL MORNING. There were times I thought the trail would never stop going up!"

The men enthusiastically confirmed Misplaced's observation. "Just when you think you're at the top, you realize you're not,"

Strength commented. Wisdom added, "You're almost at the top, but not quite there yet. It seems like you're always almost at the top." "It can get really frustrating," Misplaced replied. "There are times I think I can't climb another step."

Misplaced's comment sat wrong with Strength. "Misplaced, you're stronger than you think. You've come this far and, though it hasn't been easy, you really have done well. Sure, you've had to stop and rest, to drink and eat and breathe. But you keep going! That's what matters. I know there are times when you question whether you can make it to the top, or even why you chose to do this, but I've seen you overcome things. I've seen you make progress. I know you can do this, and you'll be thankful that you did when you get to the reward at the top of this mountain. You're about to see views that are only seen by the folks who take the hard road, who strap on a pack and walk over mountains for miles. That's significant. I really feel like you underestimate yourself, Misplaced. There's more strength in you than you realize. And this path will only make you stronger."

Though he tried to hide it, Misplaced was happy that his friend saw him in this light. He had never fit well with the athletic crowd, and Misplaced really treasured any accolades he received from folks like Strength. His friend's comments spoke to Misplaced beyond his struggle with the trail itself, and he pondered them as they continued to hike after lunch.

"I do love those views," Misplaced thought. "I really want to see more of them." As they reached the next vista, Misplaced felt that he was designed to stand on these high places, to gaze out at mountains and valleys, to see things from a different perspective. Looking out over the landscape, he felt perfectly placed.

7

Where Exactly Are We?

Misplaced, Strength, and Wisdom hiked together a while after lunch. The other men were quicker than Misplaced and he tried his best to keep up with them. As the hikers came to another hill to climb, Strength looked back at Misplaced and Wisdom, cried "Attack the hill!", and charged up the incline as fast as he could. The other men looked at one another, rolled their eyes, and followed suit. "Who's more crazy — the guy who runs up a mountain or the guy who follows him?" Misplaced thought to himself. The men gathered again at the ridgeline and started down the other side of the hill. "I'm going to run down it," Wisdom announced. "It's easier on my knees." "Is this a hike or a run?!?" Misplaced asked. Strength and Wisdom chuckled . . . and ran on. Misplaced shook his head and followed his friends downhill. "Don't turn an ankle. Don't turn an ankle. Don't turn an ankle."

With each mile that carried the men deeper into the forest, Misplaced became less certain about where he actually was. He did zero research for this trip. In fact, the only real facts he knew about the trail were that it followed a river, it led from Here to There, and that Faith had hiked it once before. He knew the name of the river that ran alongside the trail, but he knew nothing about it, except that Loyalty used to raft down the whitewater rated sections years ago.

Misplaced had never been very good with keeping his bearings. He was always confounded when he would ask for directions and be met with, "Yeah, just go east on highway 47 for about five miles. When you come to the intersection of state road 22, head north for two miles. The place you're looking for will be on the right." When it came to making turns, Misplaced navigated more by landmarks than by the compass. "Go east? Why not turn right? Head north? Can't you just say 'bear left at such-and-such store'?"

Though his mind wasn't trained to stay oriented to north and south, Misplaced was no stranger to a map. He grew up seeing atlases in the floorboards of his uncle's vehicles. They were in the farm machinery business and traveled from state to state buying and selling equipment. Misplaced heard them talk about the places they went and the people they knew there. When he would see an atlas in the truck, he wondered where they had been and where they were going next.

When he learned to drive, Misplaced wanted to hit the road. He met friends from other cities through his involvement with church camps, and he loved to drive and visit them. Following his uncles' example, he bought an atlas and left it in his car. He loved to study it before heading out on a trip, trying to find the most efficient route to his destination. He wandered up and down the highway in the days before smartphones and turn-by-turn navigation. Misplaced learned to find Point B by plotting a course, stopping for directions, and often getting turned around. "The best way to learn your way around a town is to get good and lost a few times," he often said.

On this trip, however, he had not seen a map before he was on the trail. He felt like he was hiking north, but that may not have been the case. This trail ran along the border of two states. He thought he was in one state, but he may have actually been in the other. Though he was uncertain of his whereabouts, he actually wasn't worried at all. Misplaced felt comfortable following Faith's leadership. Though he didn't know the man well, something about his demeanor made it easy for Misplaced to trust him. He was also reassured by the amount of preparation that Wisdom had done before the trip. While Misplaced was clueless about his location, Wisdom brought maps of various types and sizes.

One was a topographical map, with concentric, misshapen circles to represent mountains. Misplaced remembered learning about "topo" maps in school, but he never had a reason to use one. Another map looked like someone had straightened out the trail, cut it longways, and laid out a cross section of the mountains. This map displayed every rise and fall of the trail, complete with elevation measurements.

Wisdom had done more research than anyone else, but he was not the only hiker who planned for navigation. Faith consulted a hiking guidebook that he used when plotting his first hike from Here to There. A gadget-lover, Loyalty installed a mapping application on his phone and was following a route shared by another user.

Every time the men would stop and break for food or water, the navigators would pull out the maps of various denominations and study their progress. Misplaced was so engrossed in his own journey that he was not overly interested in the maps. The details weren't very exciting to him. As long as he saw another blaze ahead, he felt confident and was happy to keep hiking. All he needed was one more blaze.

After climbing a significantly difficult hill, the men followed the trail down to a bottom and found a confusing variety of blazes on the trees. Blue blazes headed one direction, green blazes headed another, and white blazes approached from behind. As the navigators broke out their maps to translate the blazes, the other men sat down and took advantage of the break.

"We're supposed to follow the blue blazes," Loyalty reminded everyone.

"I know, but the map shows that we follow the green blazes from this point. The green blazes should take us the rest of the way There." Wisdom responded.

"Then where do the blue blazes go now?" Loyalty asked.

"They must go down to the river. Maybe there's an overlook or something," Wisdom conjectured.

"I remember a waterfall somewhere close to here," said Faith. "I bet those blazes go to it."

"What about the white blazes?" Loyalty asked.

"There's a pretty famous trail that joins this one and follows it for quite a ways. In fact, it continues beyond There. I'm pretty sure that's it," Wisdom answered.

The men agreed that they should follow the green blazes the rest of the way There, but they would take a few minutes to see where the blue blazes led at this confusing intersection. The resting men stood up and joined them as they meandered down the blue-blazed trail, leaving their hiking packs on the ground where they stopped. After fifty yards or so, the trail led to a rocky outcropping that overlooked a beautiful waterfall. The men took turns posing for pictures with the rushing water behind them. The river was incredibly wide where the waterfall dropped into it. It appeared as though another river joined the one the trail had followed. The confluence created a rushing, churning body of water. "Certainly this is one of the spots Loyalty rafted through years ago," Misplaced thought to himself.

Once the men were finished snapping keepsake photos on their phones, they eased back up the trail to the spot where they stopped to rest and consult maps. The hikers strapped their backpacks on again and followed the green blazes away from the waterfall. The trail ran alongside a muddy creek and followed an old Jeep road.

As they walked along, Misplaced began to talk with Wisdom about his research and map reading skills.

"If you had not brought your maps, I would have been completely lost back there," Misplaced commented.

"I really enjoyed researching for the trip. I tend to be that way about anything I do. We can talk about college football, if you want. I study that, too," Wisdom said.

Misplaced was not really surprised with Wisdom's thoroughness. Being a physician, Wisdom had to be a man who enjoyed studying and running down answers to problems. "Do you know exactly where we are, Wisdom?" Misplaced asked. "You should be able to find our location pretty well on the map, now that we've passed such a significant landmark."

"Yeah, I know where we are. I'm not using an app like the one Loyalty has, so without landmarks I sometimes lose track of exactly how far we've gone. But as of right now, I have us located."

"That's cool. I'm glad you guys are staying on top of those details. I'm pretty much following you guys and walking from one blaze to the next. Without the blazes, I'd be lost. I just don't have enough navigational skills to be able to make it without them. I'd lose my bearings after the first turn in the trail and be lost."

Wisdom pondered Misplaced's comment before responding. "You know, Misplaced, I did put quite a bit of time in studying our route before we came out here. It was fun reading the maps and looking up blog posts from folks who have hiked this trail. But in all reality, once you get out here, the blazes are what get you from Here to There. In fact, they're really all you need. Somebody who knows exactly how to get There put these blazes here for us to follow. My maps show me where we started and where we'll end. I can see how the trail will twist and turn through the woods. But now that we're out here, I can only successfully navigate from one blaze to the next. That's really what we're all doing, even if we've poured over the maps ahead of time. Once our boots are on the trail and we're surrounded by trees, we don't have a birds-eye view like the maps show us. We have a limited perspective. We all walk as far as we can see, look for the next blaze, then walk a little farther. That's how you complete a journey like this."

"That would drive my wife crazy!" Misplaced joked. "She would need more information than just the next blaze."

"I know. I like more info than that, too. But sometimes that's all we have," Wisdom replied.

"I'm OK with that, but that might be because I trust you guys," said Misplaced. "Or it might be because that's how I've lived for the past few years . . . only being able to see a few feet in front of me at the time."

"We all know what that feels like," said Wisdom. "But I'm glad there's a path to follow. I'd much rather be following the blazes than bushwhacking through who-knows-what."

As Misplaced thought about Wisdom's comments, he saw him for the first time as a business-owner, not just a physician. "He doesn't just see patients," he thought. "He has to pay employees, manage the books, pay rent . . . just like me." As Misplaced hiked, he realized that most of his fellow travelers managed a business of some sort. Though he often felt like his trials were unique, he was beginning to wonder if that was not the case.

The men continued to travel down the dirt path and Misplaced continued to ponder the correlations between his hike and his experience as an entrepreneur. "When this all started, I thought I was following a path. Now I'm not so sure," Misplaced thought to himself. Surrounded by the worries and struggles of his business, Misplaced had lost his bearings, and he felt like he was walking from one crisis to the next.

"I wonder how far we are from There," he questioned. "I'm starting to wonder if I'll ever get There after all." Even in his own thoughts, Misplaced wasn't sure if he was talking about his hike or his life in general.

8

Peanut Butter and Hatchets

After leaving the waterfall, the trail followed the Jeep road as it meandered through the trees. "Whoever cut this trail didn't make it any harder on themselves than they had to," Misplaced thought. "The trail follows the river, or Jeep roads, or ridges. If I was making a trail through the forest, I'd do the same thing. It almost seems like the trail wants to be there." As these thoughts rolled around in his head, he began to think about the language of the trail and how it has crept into everyday vocabulary . . . words like "trailblazer" or phrases like, "Where in the blue blazes are we?" These words held a new meaning for him now.

The route that the trail followed seemed to be easier than it had been so far. The men hiked at a faster pace, partly because the elevation didn't change as much and partly because they were finding their "hiking legs," falling into a rhythm that helped them keep moving. As often happens late in the day, silence found its way into the crevices of the hikers' conversations. Tired bodies made for tired minds and the men focused less on chatter and more on the distance to the next campsite, which also contributed to their quickened pace. They checked and rechecked maps and apps, determining location and remaining mileage. The autumn afternoon was shorter among the trees; shadows began to creep across the forest floor long before actual sunset. As the light settled behind the treeline, a low-level anxiety settled on the hikers. Everything felt a bit heavier as the men raced sunlight toward camp, still an inexact distance away.

As he hiked along, Misplaced found that his pack required periodic adjustment. It was amazing how it could feel so foreign and at the same time so functional. Step after step, hour after hour, the weight of the pack settled into the shoulder straps. The resulting ache reminded him of high school and his trusty book bag, which he filled beyond intended capacity in an attempt to avoid stops at the locker. His borrowed hiking pack was considerably different, however. The hip belt was a game-changer. Though it felt awkward at first, he found that it allowed him to carry the weight of the pack much more comfortably than expected. Loyalty showed him how the hip belt was meant to be strapped high on the hips. The load was really carried there, not on the shoulders. "The shoulder straps shouldn't dig into your shoulders. They're really only meant to stop the pack from falling backward. Keep the hip belt tight and let it hold up the weight." However, the belt wriggled and stretched with the repeated steps, desperately looking for an opportunity to set down the load. When the familiar pain in his shoulders drew attention to the slackened hip belt, Misplaced would stop to readjust. The process looked a bit silly. He leaned forward and took a little hop; this bounced the pack enough to get the hip belt higher on his torso. When it cleared the top of his hips, Misplaced pulled the excess strap and tightened the belt. As he cinched it just a little past what felt natural, his belly protruded over the top. "Not flattering, but it gets the job done," he thought to himself. Misplaced inherited his grandfather's square frame. As a result, the waistline of his pants rode well below his high hips, much lower than the spot where the hip belt of the pack needed to rest. "These broad, high hips actually work pretty well carrying a hiking pack," he thought to himself.

The men trekked along as the trail eventually left the Jeep road and began to rise again. Pines, hardwoods, rhododendrons . . . while the scenery was beautiful, the mounting pressure to find the campsite stole from its wonder. The path hugged the side of the mountain, avoiding sharp inclines or descents. As a result, the trail took a circuitous route that multiplied necessary steps as well as available views. Misplaced and his friends were distributed out along the footpath, dotting the landscape as it wrapped around a curve in the hillside halfway between a hardwood bottom and the ridge above. Misplaced found spots like this particularly beautiful. The autumn leaves had abandoned many trees, creating views that reached through the empty spaces and much further into the distance than would have been possible in full foliage. He loved autumn; it held many fond memories for him. Growing up in the rural American south, Misplaced often spent fall mornings watching the sun come up while waiting for an elusive white tailed deer to step out of the underbrush. The brisk air and forest sounds brought to mind the most precious memories he had with this stepdad. An avid hunter, he taught Misplaced the skills of a traditional outdoorsman. Most of their quality time came in the form of hunting and this hiking trip reminded Misplaced how much he enjoyed being outdoors. He and his stepdad spent more hours preparing to hunt and cleaning up afterwards than they did on the hunt itself; Misplaced suspected that hiking would be a similar experience. Scouring maps, researching gear, packing and repacking threatened to take more time than the trip itself. If backpacking was anything like deer hunting, enthusiasts did not bemoan the time nor expense that came with preparation. It was a part that made up the whole, another element that made the experience so enjoyable. "This feels like cheating. I get to enjoy being in the woods, but I don't have to drag a deer out or dress it afterwards. I'll just walk out the other end and head home. After taking a shower and putting my gear away, I'm done," Misplaced thought to himself. He felt his stepdad would be disappointed that he was relieved not to harvest an animal and do all the work that followed. However, he felt that in a moment of honesty he would probably relate. As long as he could remember, Misplaced watched his stepdad take every opportunity he could to be outside. Deep down, he was certain it was more than the sport of hunting. Though not a "tree hugger," Misplaced knew his stepdad loved nature and had instilled this affection in him.

The hikers rounded a turn in the trail and found a convenient rocky spot to sit and rest their weary feet. Wisdom and Loyalty shed their boots and rummaged through homemade first aid kits. "I'm getting some hot spots," Loyalty announced. "What does that mean?" Misplaced asked. "A hot spot is a place where a blister will form if you don't do something to prevent it," Loyalty answered. Doctor Wisdom provided more detailed information. "Blisters are formed from repeated friction in the same spot. There are things you can do to prevent them; it really starts with your choice of socks and boots. But if you feel a hot spot coming up while hiking, you can put a piece of moleskin on it and keep it from turning into a blister." He held up what looked like a tan piece of felt cut in the shape of an oval. "Do you need any moleskin, Misplaced?" Surprisingly, his cotton socks and running shoes had served him well so far. "No, I think I'm OK. My feet are tired, but they feel good."

"My feet are definitely telling me that I packed too much!" Loyalty retorted. The men chuckled as they commented on their friend's large rucksack filled with a variety of items which had been proven unnecessary in utility or quantity. Lingering to tend sore feet, the men pulled out trail mix and crackers, taking the opportunity to refuel as they rested. As Misplaced dug in his pack for something to eat, he noticed the jar of peanut butter he brought from home, which now seemed inexcusably heavy. "Why didn't I scoop some out into a plastic bag? Did I think I'd eat the whole jar out here?" he asked himself. It was amazing how much he had learned about hiking from just two days of lugging his pack along the trail. Misplaced couldn't pass up the opportunity to confess his rookie mistakes and commiserate with Loyalty. "I bet most of us packed something we really didn't need. I know I did! Check this out!" He held up his jar of peanut butter as his friends erupted in laughter. "You think that's heavy? Look at this . . . " Misplaced reached deep into his pack and pulled out the collapsible hatchet he purchased from the Army-Navy surplus store especially for this trip. "Feel this!" He passed the implement around the convoy so the men could take turns commenting in jest. When he had gone "car camping" in the past, Misplaced kept a hatchet in his gear to chop large limbs or drive tent stakes into hard ground. After his first night in a backcountry campsite, he realized he didn't get enough use out of his new hatchet to justify carrying the extra weight.

As the hatchet made its way around the circle of men, Faith commented. "It really is funny how your definition of 'necessary equipment' changes after you have to carry it for a day or two . . . and haven't used it once!" Resolve responded, "Right? Some stuff seems like it would be obviously helpful but really isn't — like the hatchet. Other stuff seems silly but ends up being really useful — like my chair." Resolve pointed to the aluminum folding chair strapped to the outside of his pack. "I know it looks ridiculous and you think you can just sit on a rock or log at camp, but it weighs nothing and I want to sit in a chair with a back after a long day of hiking." The men commented in agreement, most wishing they had thought to bring a chair as well.

Strength spoke up, "Misplaced, I gave you a hard time about your pack when we left home, but looking around it seems that we all struggled to know what to bring and what to leave behind. It makes me think of my clients at the gym. It's amazing to see how much better a person can perform after losing just ten pounds of unnecessary weight. Cut out twenty or thirty pounds and it's a night-and-day difference. We would all be able to hike further or faster and have a lot more fun doing it if we made better decisions about what weight we need to carry and what we should leave at home. When I was sticking things in this pack, I didn't realize the commitment I was making! I know that I would pack differently if I was doing it now. I'd be a lot more careful about the weight that I choose to carry. I'd get rid of anything I didn't need. Trying to carry unnecessary weight could keep any of us from getting There."

Chattering in agreement, the men began to stand and secure their packs, readying themselves for the remaining miles of the day. Misplaced had gotten pretty good at grabbing his pack by the straps and slinging it around onto his back. As he buckled his hip belt and tightened the load lifters on the shoulder straps, Misplaced thought about the weight he was carrying. Some things were necessary and helpful, others were not. Some of the items he packed were carefully considered, others he carried because someone else said he should, and certain things ended up in his pack with very little thought at all. Regardless of how this hodge-podge of "equipment" ended up on his back, he now had to carry it. All of it. There was no use begrudging his decisions at this point; he would know better how to pack for the next trip, should there ever be one. In the meantime, he had to bear the load he chose and keep walking the trail before him.

The men walked in a tight line for a few hundred yards before the procession began to stretch out and settle into a slow and steady rhythm toward evening camp. As Misplaced walked along, he felt the weight he was carrying on his back and in his mind. Like his backpacking gear, Misplaced was aware that he was carrying a variety of heavy burdens that threatened to keep him from reaching his destination. Some he picked up along the way because they seemed necessary, like the Lone Ranger self-defense mechanism. He was beginning to see that it was more hindrance than help. Other burdens were acquired because someone else told him they were necessary, like his nagging student loans. However, some things that weighed heavily upon him were loads he carried with joy, knowing that he was intended to bear them. As he hiked along, he thought fondly about his wife and children. His business would have had no hope of success if his wife had not been such an incredible spouse, partner, and leader. Misplaced thought about the countless nights when he felt he was suffocating under the business and found that holding one of his children brought comfort and relief. He certainly carried a burden for his family, to lead and provide for them. If there was any necessary weight, anything he should carry that would help him make it There, it was these precious relationships. As Misplaced looked down the trail at the line of men who were quickly becoming brothers, he realized that he needed to shed some unhelpful burdens so he could pick up some necessary ones. "I've isolated myself long enough," Misplaced thought to himself. He quickened his pace to catch up to Loyalty, happy not to be walking alone.

9

One Big Hill

The trail and river lingered together like two friends enjoying a long chat, in no hurry to part ways. The overgrowth indicated that most people didn't follow the route this far, likely reversing in return to the trailhead from which the group departed. Despite the brush encroaching onto the single-track path, the walking was actually easier. As long as the trail ran beside the river, the elevation didn't change dramatically. This wouldn't last for long.

As is the case when the trail hugs the river, small wooden bridges traversed tributaries along this section, flowing from the mountainside into the river below. Though the rushing water was not calm, its sound certainly was. Because the trail evacuated the forest canopy to play alongside the water, the men traded the shade for full sunlight. Misplaced found that the warmth of the sun and the sound of the river lifted his mood even higher. He was very happy on the trail, happier than he had felt in months . . . or even years.

As the official trip planner, Faith did his best to prepare the men for what the journey might hold. This trail was not particularly historic, nor was it part of the national long trail just a few miles up the road. As a result, there were only a few detailed maps published for this route and scarce online resources. Even if a wealth of information had been available, most of the novice hikers had no interest in researching the trail itself. Just gathering the correct gear was overwhelming; they were happy to follow Faith as he led the way into the unknown.

When Faith described the trail, he did so with comforting words. "It's not a very difficult trail. There's only one big hill," he often repeated. This description emboldened the hikers as they anticipated their first real backcountry trip. However, the statement had become a joke among the tiring backpackers.

"Hey Faith! Was the last hill the 'one big hill,' or was it the one before that?!?" prodded Resolve.

"I sure am glad there's only ONE big hill on this trail. Otherwise I'd be really tired right now," said an exhausted Loyalty.

The cohort had once again spread out as they followed the trail along the river. In fact, Misplaced couldn't spot anyone up ahead. "I hear them, but they're nowhere to be seen!" he thought. "A maintenance team really should come out this far and clean up the underbrush," Misplaced commented under his breath as he tried to identify the trail before him. It seemed to disappear into a wall of green and brown vegetation.

"Hey Misplaced! Up here! Remember that one big hill???" Faith called from above. "Here it is!" Misplaced looked in the direction of his friend's voice and saw that the trail made a hairpin turn to the left away from the river . . . and UP! As his eyes followed the path, he saw Faith waiting in the shadows and directing the way. Misplaced peered further up the mountain, noticing another figure that seemed to be floating among the trees. It was Wisdom, further up the trail. "Where does this thing go?!?" Misplaced wondered to himself. He leaned forward and began the slow ascent toward Faith.

When Misplaced reached his friend, he realized that he was standing in the corner of another turn, next to a tree with two blazes. "See how these two blazes are offset? This means the trail is making a hard turn," Faith explained. Sure enough, the trail made another hairpin turn, this time to the right. "The trail turns like this so you don't have to walk straight up the side of the mountain to get to the ridge at the top. Look up there — can you imagine how hard it would be to hike up that incline?" Misplaced looked toward the ridge above, hidden by the densely wooded hillside. "Yeah, I would NOT want to do that!" he replied.

The path zig-zagged its way up the mountain. "These are called switchbacks, when the trail turns like this," Faith explained. "I'm thankful for whoever cut them," replied Misplaced. "It takes a lot more steps to get to the top, but I'd much rather do it this way. I don't know if I could make it going straight up the side." Misplaced was struggling to breathe as he made the slow ascent, even with the help of the switchbacks.

Faith and Misplaced walked and talked as they made their way up the "one big hill." The trail made turn after turn, left then right then left again. At almost every switchback, Misplaced stopped a minute to let his heart rate recover before making the next gradual but challenging climb. The turns provided a natural series of attainable goals.

The trek up the hill reminded Misplaced of being newly married and jogging around the neighborhood with his wife, Mosey. She had never done any distance running before and found the practice frustrating. While jogging, her motivation faded quickly and she would announce, "I can't do it anymore! I'm walking!" At this, Misplaced would goad her on, "See that mailbox just up ahead? Run there and then we'll stop." Once the slow pair of runners reached the mailbox, Misplaced would say, "Feel OK? Don't stop now, run to the next one!" Mosey would roll her eyes, huff at Misplaced, and run a little further. One mailbox after another, the two made their way around the neighborhood and back to their driveway.

"Just make it to the next switchback," Misplaced told himself. "You can rest there." Turn after turn, Misplaced and Faith continued to follow the trail up the mountainside. Despite their sparse autumn foliage, the trees blocked the afternoon sun. When he stopped to rest, Misplaced found that he cooled down quickly. "I thought I'd be cold out here, but I'm really comfortable in shorts and a t-shirt as long as I'm walking. I don't get cold until I stop for a while," he commented to Faith.

When the pair finally reached the ridgeline, they found Wisdom and Strength waiting at the top. "Glad you made it!" Strength teased. "Have you seen Resolve and Loyalty?" Wisdom asked. "They're behind us a-ways. They'll be here shortly," Faith answered.

The men leaned on their trekking poles, chatting as they awaited their companions. Though they were higher in elevation, the ridge exposed the hikers to the sun and they found themselves enjoying its warmth as they rested.

Loyalty and Resolve turned the last switchback and soon after emerged out of the forest. The waiting hikers stood at attention and adjusted their packs, preparing to resume the trek. "Oh, I see how this works," complained Loyalty. "The slowpokes who obviously need a break don't get it because you jokers are all rested up and ready to go! Not so fast! Give us a minute." The others chuckled and agreed to linger a bit longer so their friends could recover from the punishing ascent.

"So that was the 'one big hill,' huh Faith?" teased Resolve. "That one was definitely the biggest, but I wouldn't call the others 'small' by any means," added Wisdom.

"Yeah, so maybe there was more than one big hill along the way," responded Faith. "It has been a while since I hiked this trail and this was the only hill that really stood out in my memory," he continued.

"It's probably because it's the only one that has switchbacks like that," said Resolve. "No other hill so far has had a change in elevation that required them."

"Now that you mention it, I think you're right," Faith replied. "This one was certainly challenging, but it wasn't the only hard climb we've faced so far."

"It's funny to me that you forgot all the other hills before this one," commented Misplaced. "It's like this one hill totally eclipsed all the other ones."

"I remember different things about the trail as we are hiking it," said Faith. "Things I couldn't remember at home. Certain stretches along the river, or a vista on the ridgeline, or even a particular bridge across a stream . . . they come back to mind when we get to them. I talked about the 'one big hill' a lot, but every hill between Here and There makes up the journey, and every hill has its own challenges. I tell you, when I'm hiking up them, I'm hurting and I'm certain I'll remember every step because they're all painful. But I don't. You guys won't either. You'll see . . . when we get There and this journey is over, so much of the pain will fade and you'll remember the trip differently. You'll remember all the epic stuff about it, not so much the hurt it inflicted on you."

"I don't know," retorted Loyalty. "I'm not entirely sure why we gave up a weekend to come out here and hurt ourselves for fun! It's kind of crazy that we call this recreation!"

"I read somewhere that every hiker asks himself that question all the way up the mountain," said Wisdom, "and swears to sell all his gear when he gets home."

"It's true," replied Faith. "But I bet we'll be planning the next trip before we pull back in our driveways! And when you find yourself staring up a big hill on another hike, you'll remember how you climbed this one and you won't be so afraid. Speaking of heading home . . . should we get a move on?" The men mumbled in agreement and proceeded along the ridgeline.

For Misplaced, the entrepreneurial journey held one challenge after another with very little rest between. Though this hiking trip was physically demanding, it was a reprieve from the mental and emotional demands of his business. Faith's words sparked a tiny thought of hope in his mind. "I wonder if I'll get to the point where I don't remember all the pain that owning a business has caused me," he wondered. "Will the benefits ever outweigh the costs?" He imagined that most of his friends and family probably thought of his decision to open a business much like they thought of this hiking trip: "Why in the world would anyone do that?!?" From the ridgeline Misplaced could see miles of wooded mountains and valleys. The view brought to mind Strength's words from earlier in the day. "The only way to see what I'm looking at right now is to walk the path that I just walked. You can't drive here and just jump out of a car. You have to climb that 'one big hill' to see this view," Misplaced thought to himself. "There aren't a lot of people who have seen what I'm looking at right now, and all of them have endured the same pain that I did to get here." In that moment, Misplaced was proud to count himself among the people who had chosen to travel such a difficult path, and equally thankful for the breathtaking view it provided.

10

In the Light of the Campfire

The procession of hikers followed the ridge as the trail meandered beneath the bare skeletal canopy. The afternoon light was a somber mixture of gold and grey, pressing the men toward camp as the sun descended behind the trees. At a large stand of pines, the trail plunged from the ridge into a wet, shadowy bottom. After several hours of walking through the highlands without easy access to water, they were not going to pass up an opportunity to filter and fill their bottles. After a brief respite, the men donned their packs and proceeded along the way.

The path was muddy as it left the bottom and remained flat for the rest of the afternoon, refusing to climb another hill. Winding their way out of the dense woods, the hikers were relieved to walk in a spacious place. Trees were more gratuitously distributed, allowing the fading rays to reach the forest floor. The men continued to cross trickling creeks and eventually heard the rush of the river.

"Where are we camping tonight?" Though it was not specifically addressed, Strength directed his question toward Faith. "I'm not entirely sure. On the last trip, I think we camped in that bottom where we stopped for water. I believe the trailhead is just a few miles from here; if I'm right, we're almost There! Let's go ahead and find a good spot next to the river and call it a day." Everyone happily agreed. It had been a long day of hiking, covering more miles than anticipated. The men were ready to rest until morning.

The trail turned to the left and drew near the river. "This looks like a good spot. Want to stop here?" Wisdom asked. "Looks like camp to me!" replied Faith.

The site had plenty of space for the six hikers. The lack of underbrush and presence of a stone fire ring indicated that it had been utilized by backpackers many times before. Each man chose a homestead and began setting up shelter. Misplaced pitched his tiny dirt dauber tent between Loyalty and the trail. Exhausted from the long day's hike, he climbed in the tent to rest. He stretched out in the orange cocoon with just a few inches of clearance between himself and the tent wall on any side. In a sudden shock of excruciating pain, his hamstring wrenched into a cramp. Misplaced frantically fought his way out of the tent, almost tearing it down in the process. He stood up and attempted to walk off the cramp, nearly fainting as the blood rushed from his head to aid the injured muscle.

"Are you OK?" Loyalty asked. Misplaced answered his concerned neighbor as he limped around the campsite, "Got a cramp in my leg . . . I'll be alright in a minute." He hobbled in circles but the charley horse was persistent, refusing to relent. As he continued to grimace in pain, Loyalty offered advice. "If I were you, I'd jump in the river. The cold water will help ease off the cramp." Misplaced was reluctant to take what seemed to be such a drastic measure, but the pain was an effective motivator. He managed to squeak out a thankful response, "OK. I'll give it a try."

Misplaced gingerly shed his shirt and shoes, careful to keep his leg positioned so that the contraction would not repeat. He limped to the bank of the river and eased himself into the icy water. Gasping for air, he slowly sunk into the current and leaned back to float while nature provided cryotherapy for his pitiful legs. Sure enough, the cramp subsided. "How does that feel?" Loyalty asked from the bank. "Sure is cold, but it feels good. Thanks!" Misplaced responded gratefully.

After ten minutes of relief, Misplaced waded out of the water and braced for another cold shock as the breeze accosted his exposed skin. While he was nursing his injury, the other hikers gathered wood and started a campfire. Motivated by the fire's warm invitation, Misplaced quickly dried off, changed into his camp clothes, and joined his friends. Logs were positioned strategically around the fire ring to serve as benches. Men were distributed equidistant around the stone circle, rifling through their cooking gear as they prepared dinner. They happily chatted while the sunlight gave way to the darkness of night.

Normally, campfires had a meditative quality for Misplaced. He was typically soothed by the crackling sound. Usually, the light would draw his attention and he would spend hours entertained by the flames. However, Misplaced was infinitely exhausted and found very little comfort in the campfire. He identified with the logs as they dried up and crumbled into embers this evening.

His companions were in much better spirits. Devouring bowls of chili mac and ramen noodles, they bantered about a variety of topics. They shared anecdotes from marriage, fatherhood, friendship, and business, volleying witty comments and laughing as the evening grew older. Loyalty turned the conversation in a spiritual direction, offering some thoughts from a recent bible study at church. The subject was welcomed and the men took turns commenting. Strength contributed to the discussion and Wisdom responded with particularly helpful insight. Faith affirmed the thoughts that had been shared and supported them with quotations from scripture. Resolve gave a personal testimony on the topic. In the meantime, Misplaced sat and listened, conspicuously quiet.

He could not tell which was more fatigued, his body or his mind. As the friends continued their discussion, Misplaced was deeply bothered by his complete indifference to the subject. Perhaps it was actually his spirit that was the most exhausted.

For decades, Christian faith was his favorite topic of conversation. Tonight, however, Misplaced had nothing to contribute to the discussion. His apathy was most disturbing, made apparent to himself by his failure to engage. On other evenings, fellowship by the fire had offered peace, relief, and joy. Tonight, Misplaced found himself exposed by the light of the campfire, ashamed at the condition of his soul. Though no one else noticed, he could not ignore what he saw in himself. Misplaced was weak, weary, and spiritually anemic. While tending to the incessant needs of his business, he had neglected his inner life. He wished he could claim it was an unintentional error, but Misplaced new better.

Entrepreneurship was the hardest endeavor that Misplaced had undertaken to date, and he resented the difficulty it imposed upon him. He feared that it robbed his family, rerouting his attention and affections to the business and away from his wife and children. He was certain it had damaged friendships. How did he end up in this condition?

In a moment of honesty, Misplaced realized that he had been angry with God about his business. He knew that God called him to walk this path, but it was much more difficult than he expected. Others had warned him, but their words could not prepare him for the experience. He had lost perspective in an attempt to merely survive, and in his campfire contemplation Misplaced wondered if he was surviving at all. What if his business pulled through, but his faith did not? He found his identity in Jesus, but now he struggled to identify with anything except his business. He felt lost and disoriented, uncertain of who he was or where he was headed.

As he faced the reality of his condition, his friends' chatter faded into the background with the evening sounds of the forest. Misplaced stared at the throbbing embers of the campfire and realized that this was a significant moment, a turning point, a line in the sand. In his mind he made a declaration of discontentment, a decision that would alter his trajectory from this point forward.

"I am ashamed that I ended up Here, but I will not stay Here. I will never be in this place again."

If he was going to make it from Here to There, Misplaced realized he needed to make some hard decisions. The first one was to prioritize his inner life — his relationship with God, his spiritual health, his personal growth, the condition of his soul. He needed to remember who God called him to be, not just what God called him to do. In his attempt to be successful as an entrepreneur, he risked becoming a failure as a human being. Misplaced decided then and there to recover a renewed vision for his life and start growing.

11

Always Misplaced

The campfire discussion continued until late evening when the men began to turn in for their last night in the backcountry. Heavy with self-reflection, Misplaced was one of the first to retire. He washed his cooking implements, stowed them away, and crawled into his miniscule tent.

Evening well-wishes passed between sleepy hikers and soon the river's voice was all that was heard. Misplaced lay on his back, bundled in the borrowed sleeping bag, staring at the roof of the tent just inches above his face. He had never considered himself claustrophobic, but the diminutive shelter seemed to be shrinking. Misplaced desperately wanted to drift off to sleep, his body practically begging for rest. Unfortunately, his mind would not cooperate and insisted on replaying hypothetical worst-case scenarios. First he worried what would happen if the leg cramp returned while he was asleep and he jumped up in pain, unaware of his surroundings. He would cause a horrible commotion as he leapt to his feet and took the tent with him! This fear transformed into another anxious preoccupation. What if a bear wandered up looking for a midnight snack and Misplaced needed to escape? He couldn't get out of the cocoon tent fast enough to flee, and would probably end up wrapped in fabric and rope as he tried frantically to exit the tiny structure. (As if outrunning a bear was a logical option to begin with!) After several minutes of slow breathing and mental gymnastics, Misplaced was able to become still enough to drift off.

The morning sun peered into the tent and Misplaced heard the early chirping of birds above the rushing river. This was one of his favorite things about camping, waking up to a cold nose and the pleasant sounds of the forest. He was comfortably warm in his sleeping bag, though his muscles were not happy with the hard ground. Misplaced never wanted to be the first person stirring at the campsite; once someone is up and about, there is an unspoken expectation that everyone else will shortly follow suit. Misplaced did not want to be the first domino to fall, so he lay and waited and thought. "I cannot sleep in a bivy tent . . . I need more space." He was intrigued by Resolve's hammock setup. "There's something about using a hammock for camping. I'll have to check that out."

Before long, the campsite came alive with the sounds of rustling leaves and boiling water. Faith stirred the campfire just enough to warm the sleepy men as they made coffee and breakfast. "I think we're not far from There. Maybe an hour and half of hiking and we'll be out," he announced. Though they moved slowly, the hikers were eager to break camp and finish the trip. "This has been fun, but I'm ready for a hot meal and a shower," thought Misplaced.

Tents were packed and the fire extinguished; the companions stood in a circle and chatted as Loyalty and Wisdom made their final preparations before striking out. When the last packs were strapped on, Faith asked Strength to say a prayer as they started the final leg of the journey. Giving thanks for safety and friendship, the men turned their attention to There and started walking.

Conversations ebbed and flowed as the six friends progressed toward their destination. The trail ran alongside the river until it came to a long metal bridge spanning to the other bank. Each man tarried a moment as he crossed, taking in the wild beauty of the water and the woods.

The trail continued along the opposite side of the river in the other direction, then diverted just far enough into the forest to lose sight of the water. Before long the occasional sound of a vehicle was heard above the rushing current and the men knew they were approaching the highway and the trailhead There.

Having spread out during the final hike, the men emerged from the forest in pairs. Misplaced and Loyalty walked out of the shade of the trees to shouts of celebration from the other side of the highway. Their companions stood around the vehicle that had been deposited at the trailhead two days earlier and cheered as hikers reached their destination.

It was done. The six men had successfully completed their epic journey. Misplaced quickly shed his pack, glad to be relieved of the burden that he carried from Here to There. As had become his custom, he leaned on his hiking staff while he laughed with his fellow adventurers and lingered in the moment. Cars crossed the highway bridge over the river and Misplaced thought about how far he had come in his three-day trek from Here to There. Though this journey had come to an end, he had the feeling that it was the first of many to follow.

As the men packed their gear into the vehicle and prepared to head home, Misplaced sensed that something significant had happened . . . or had begun to happen. The difficult path from Here to There had blessed him with many surprising gifts. He had a renewed perspective on the life waiting for him at home. When he stepped foot into his business on Monday, could he dare to believe that it was another challenging journey promising unforeseen rewards? Could it be another difficult path leading him to a new There, a destination that he could not imagine? Like the embers of last night's campfire, hope flickered as he entertained the thought.

"It hurts while you're hiking, but man does it feel great to look back down the trail and realize how far you've come?!?" Resolve commented. "I knew every step would hurt, and I was right. And it was totally worth it." The men laughed in agreement, lined up for a group photo, and piled into the vehicle. Faith looked back from the driver's seat and announced, "Time to plan the next trip! Where do you guys want to go from Here?"

Misplaced looked at the dirty faces of his companions and realized he was in a special fraternity, an epic brotherhood, a fellowship of suffering. He knew then that he would always be a traveler on a journey from Here to There, always walking another difficult path. He knew he would always be misplaced. Now he also knew that he would end up There, not because of his own determination, but because he would no longer walk alone.

The six hikers upon arrival There

(L-R) Wisdom, Misplaced, Strength, Resolve, Loyalty, Faith

Reflection Guide

These reflection questions will help you apply the principles from *Misplaced* to your own difficult path. I have reserved them for the end of the book so that you might enjoy the story uninterrupted. While I have attempted to provide prompts that are relevant for a wide variety of readers, I have done so assuming that all readers share one commonality: you are facing some difficult path of your own. Perhaps this is why you were curious enough to read my short little book. Or maybe you began reading and only then realized that you relate to Misplaced. Before you work through the reflection questions, take a moment to complete the following sentences:

My difficult path is . . .
It is difficult because . . .

Don't sugarcoat the situation. This is your place to vent and complain. Chances are, no one will read your notes except you.

I have endeavored to write this book in such a way that it honestly reflects my own journey, in which Christian faith has played a leading role. I hope I have written in such a way that the story honestly presents the significance of Christianity in my life while also being accessible and enjoyable for non-Christian readers. Though this book is not a bible study nor devotional literature, I have listed a few passages of scripture from the Christian Bible at the end of each chapter's reflection questions. I have not included any personal commentary on these passages. If you are so inclined, I invite you to read them, and allow them to speak for themselves.

My hope and expectation is that you will hear the still, small voice of the Holy Spirit as you do so.

A word about community. While you may prefer to process the story and the reflection questions alone, consider reading and responding with a group of friends. My aim has been to write questions that would serve well in a variety of reading groups, e.g. small business staff, entrepreneur support groups, church small groups, etc. I suspect you will find extra layers of significance if you share the experience.

Read through the reflection questions for each chapter and choose the ones to which you feel like responding. You are not expected to give them equal time or attention. While space is not included to write responses, you may want to consider doing so in a journal or notebook. "Words disentangle themselves when they pass through the lips and fingertips." (Dawson Trotman)

Chapter 1: An Invitation to Go There

You have probably seen a map in a stairwell or shopping mall that says, "You are here." Consider the circumstances of your life today. Where are you? What is "Here" for you? What does it look like? Are you happy with "Here"? Or are you in a place that you need to leave?

Where are you connected in significant relationships? Would you classify yourself as an extrovert, an introvert, or somewhere in between? Do you have any tendencies that keep you isolated? If so, what are they?

Loyalty told Misplaced, "I can tell you're worn out, friend. If you're tired of being Here, you have to take a step toward There." Do his words speak to you? If so, in what way? Do you feel an invitation to leave where you are (Here) and go to a new place (There)?

Are you able to maintain significant friendships in the midst of large initiatives? If so, what is your strategy for doing so? Do your relationships suffer when you are committed to a project? If so, what tendencies usually cause the damage?

How significant are relationships for goal-oriented people?

Do you have any relationships that have been pushed aside in favor of other endeavors or distractions? If so, should you make amends? Can the relationships be restored? Do you want them to be? What would it take to do so?

"You've done the first thing — make a decision to leave Here and go There. From this point you just need to prepare as best you know how and move in that direction." If you have determined that you need to take a difficult journey of your own, to leave Here and go There, do not fall victim to "analysis paralysis." Don't overthink it. If you have experienced some small moment of clarity, leverage whatever motivation, willpower and scant preparation available and act upon it. Every epic journey starts with putting one foot in front of another. What does the first step look like for you?

Further reading: Genesis 2:15–3:9, 12:1–4; Joshua 1:1–9

Chapter 2: Preparing to Go

How are you equipped for the journey that you are facing? Are there any ways that you fear you are not adequately equipped for your difficult path?

Would you consider yourself an independent person? How is your independence healthy or unhealthy?

Misplaced described his independent nature as a survival skill. How do people use independence in this way? How do you use your independence?

Faith told Misplaced, "You have more resources than you realize to help you get from Here to There. Seek them out. Don't be afraid to ask for help." How easily do you ask for help? To whom do you go when you need help?

"Getting from Here to There seemed to be a bigger journey than [Misplaced] could navigate on his own. He was right." Who has helped you navigate life to this point? Who is helping you navigate now?

Who would help you along your difficult path if you asked? How could you initiate or restore a connection with this person?

Further reading: Ecclesiastes 4:9–12; Proverbs 16:1–3, 27:10; 1 Corinthians 12:4–20; 2 Peter 1:3–8

Chapter 3: Every Step is Going to Hurt

Resolve told Misplaced, "I made up my mind before I came on this hike that every step would be painful. But there are some long, hard, beautiful miles between Here and There, and I wanted to see all of them. It's that way with any journey like this. The only way to cover all those miles is to take one more step . . . even if it hurts." How much did you know about your difficult path before you started out?

Does the path you are on seem to be harder than you anticipated? How so?

Most people are committed to being comfortable. Resolve was committed to the journey, believing it would reward him with something worth the pain. To what are you committed? Is it worth committing to, even if it hurts?

Misplaced had no experience with hiking and, as a result, he was surprised by the difficulty. Resolve knew exactly what he was signing up for and expected it to hurt. What about you? Did you know your path would be difficult or were you caught off guard?

Consider your path. Is it worth it? Are you willing to continue walking a path that promises to hurt with every step? How could you find the resolve to do so?

Further reading: Psalm 23; Jeremiah 29:1–14; Luke 14:25–33; Philippians 4:1–13

Chapter 4: Sixty Pounds... and Then Some

When things get tough, we often become inwardly-focused. Are you paying attention to what is happening in the lives of other people around you? Have you turned inward, losing sight of people who love you? How are you celebrating others' successes during your times of struggle?

How do you handle failure? Do you tend to withdraw from others or seek their help?

How do you stay intentionally connected with others?

Consider your current state. Did you get here intentionally? If so, how? If not, can you identify the circumstances, events, and choices that brought you to where you are?

Further reading: Proverbs 18:1, 24:15–16

Chapter 5: Adapt and Overcome

What expectations keep you from thinking outside of the norm? From where do these expectations come?

Your path is inherently difficult, but the way in which you travel it can multiply and magnify its difficulty. How did you decide to travel your path the way that you do?

When was the last time you tried something new? How did it turn out?

Are you eager to experiment with new ideas? Do you avoid change? Or are you somewhere between these extremes?

How do you usually respond when you try something new and then fail?

How does your attitude toward innovation and failure affect the way you travel your difficult path?

What unnecessary difficulties might be removed from your life? What would it take to remove them? Would it be worth the effort?

What necessary difficulties need to be approached in new ways and conquered?

Further reading: Judges 6–7; Romans 12:1–2

Chapter 6: Almost to the Top (Again)

What do you think about the concept of calling? What is a "calling" and from where does it come? Is it the same thing as a career or vocation?

Do you believe you are fulfilling your calling? Why or why not?

Do you tend to take the path of least resistance? Or the path of most resistance? How has your approach to resistance impacted your life thus far?

Have you ever felt overwhelmed with the circumstances of your life? How did you handle it? Do you feel overwhelmed with your life now?

Have your choices cost you more than you intended to pay? Have they been worth it?

Do you believe that God is good, even if your life is full of difficulty and failure? Even if it doesn't make sense? Do you believe that the Holy Spirit will direct your steps?

Further reading: 1 Samuel 3; Psalm 139:13–16; Isaiah 6:1–8; Jeremiah 1:1–10; Mark 4:35–41; Luke 5:1–11, 27–32; 2 Peter 1:10–11

Chapter 7: Where Exactly Are We?

Wisdom told Misplaced, "We have a limited perspective. We all walk as far as we can see, look for the next blaze, then walk a little farther. That's how you complete a journey like this." How comfortable are you with walking "as far as [you] can see"? How does your limited perspective affect your attitude as you travel this difficult path?

Do you feel like your trials are unique? Do you know anyone else who has been through the same difficulties that you are facing?

Your path may be the most difficult one you have ever walked. Admit its difficulty. Others have walked paths as difficult as yours... or more so. This fact can bring a sense of comforting camaraderie as well as perspective. Practice admitting the difficulty you face. Say "This is hard!" Then remember those who have walked even more difficult paths and adjust your perspective by stating, "This is hard . . . for me." Be encouraged that if others have walked much harder paths and reached There, you can too.

"When this all started, I thought I was following a path. Now I'm not so sure." Do you still see the path on which you started out? Does it look different than it did before? Are you still headed in the right direction?

Do you feel as if you have lost your bearings? That you are "walking from one crisis to another"? What would help you regain your sense of direction?

While we all have limited perspectives, we benefit from the wisdom and advice of others who have walked the difficult path before us. Consider reaching out to someone who would share his/her perspective with you.

Further reading: Proverbs 4

Chapter 8: Peanut Butter and Hatchets

How do you feel at this point on your difficult path? Enthusiastic or bored? Invigorated or exhausted? What factors have contributed to your current state?

The setting sun pressured the hikers to find camp, adding to their stress. What pressures add stress to your journey? Do you have any control over them? How do you handle stressors that are out of your control?

"Hot spots" are caused by repeated friction in the same spot and, untreated, become blisters. Blisters make hiking even more painful and can take hikers off the trail. Where do you feel repeated friction in your life? What are you doing to relieve it? Unattended hot spots may cause you to forfeit your difficult path and the rewards it promises.

What are you carrying that is weighing you down? What burdens might prevent you from reaching your destination?

What burdens are you carrying that seemed necessary but now you realize are not? What burdens are you carrying because someone else said you needed them? What burdens are you carrying because they truly are necessary?

Further reading: Matthew 6:25–34, 11:28–30; Philippians 4:4–7; James 1:2–15

Chapter 9: One Big Hill

Did you research your difficult path before you set out? Or have you trusted someone else to lead the way? How has the way you started affected the difficulty of your path?

What difficulties are you facing that could be much, much harder if approached differently? Are there ways that others have helped you, even if your path still seems particularly difficult?

Do you have attainable goals along your path? Do you celebrate them? If so, how? Do you find them helpful? In what way?

How do you motivate yourself to keep going when the path gets particularly difficult?

Think about the difficulties you have faced on your journey so far. How would your journey be different if it did not include these challenges?

Have you overcome any difficulties that have helped you on your current journey? What are they and how did you surmount them? How do you think your current challenges will embolden you for future ones?

You cannot work incessantly and expect to maintain the stamina to make it There. Rest is necessary. What do you do to find reprieve from your difficult path?

What have you seen along your difficult path that is special, unique to those who choose to take such a difficult journey? Does this add any value or meaning to the challenges you have faced?

How does it make you feel to know that you are part of an elite group of people who walk such a difficult path? Who else do you know who has walked this path ahead of you? Perhaps have a conversation with them about their journey.

Further reading: Hebrews 11:1–12:13

Chapter 10: In the Light of the Campfire

*T*o get the most out of this chapter, you need to be in a "spa-cious place." This will be a place with enough room to provide distance from the things that crowd you physically, mentally and spiritually. Make time for self-evaluation. You may not have a camp-fire by which you can sit, but it is important to make space to think without distraction. Put your phone and computer away. Spend a half or whole day by yourself. It takes extended time to unplug and get in a good frame of mind for self evaluation.

How does your life compare to what it was five years ago? Are you happy with it? Where do you want to be five years from now?

Are you paying attention to your inner life? If so, how? Have you neglected your inner life? If so, what has caused the neglect? What steps can you take to place sufficient focus on your inner life?

What role have you played in getting where you are? It is easy to blame others for our circumstances; what blame do you carry?

Do you find yourself resenting the difficult path you are on? How has it cost you, your family, and your friends? Do you blame others for its difficulty? If so, whom? Yourself? Your spouse? A friend? An advisor? God?

Misplaced "felt lost and disoriented, uncertain of who he was or where he was headed." Do you relate with him? If so, in what way?

Perhaps today is a "significant moment, a turning point, a line in the sand" for you. Do you need to make a "declaration of discontentment"? If so, what should it say? Do you need to make a decision that will alter your trajectory? What might this decision be? Write it down.

Further reading: Psalm 22

Chapter 11: Always Misplaced

Do you need a new perspective regarding your difficult path? How have your reflections regarding Misplaced's story affected the way you understand your own journey?

Do you find it difficult to believe that your difficult path can yield surprising rewards? If so, what makes you skeptical that it will end well or be worth the effort?

Is there a faint flicker of hope regarding your difficult path? What can you do to fan it into flame?

Do you have "a special fraternity, an epic brotherhood, a fellowship of suffering" to walk with along your difficult path? If not, what can you do to find one?

Further reading: Ecclesiastes 7:8; Psalm 133

Epilogue

From the coffee shop to the UK

I began writing *Misplaced* just a few years after the event which it portrays. At that time, I could never have imagined where I would be when the manuscript was finally completed and submitted for publication. At the time of writing, I live in England as a postgraduate student at the University of Cambridge. How did I get from a coffee shop in Georgia to the UK? Short answer: I learned to embrace difficult journeys.

After seven years in entrepreneurship, my wife and I discerned God's leadership back to academia. We sold the café and I returned to seminary to complete the master's degree I abandoned due to the demands of business. After graduation, we sold our estate and relocated to the UK to pursue two other graduate degrees. I am currently completing a Master of Philosophy with the Faculty of Divinity at Cambridge and have been accepted as a PhD candidate with the School of Divinity at the University of St. Andrews in Scotland.

Nearing completion of this manuscript, I was surprised by two ways in which the writing of this little allegory connects with my academic research in the New Testament. First. I accidentally wrote a book which mirrors my PhD topic. Second, the process of writing this story shares many characteristics with the composition of the gospels; thoughtful consideration of this book may be helpful when reading about the life of Jesus from the Christian Bible. If you are interested in indulging a nerdy epilogical rabbit trail, I draw the parallels in a document that can be downloaded from my website. To access it, visit efosterw.com/misplaced.